THE FLIRT

Tossing her friends a smile, Melanie hurried to get in the cafeteria line behind Scott and silently rehearsed the tips for flirting as she went.

"Hi, Scott," she said sweetly. She opened her eyes wide and looked directly into his, wishing that she were wearing mascara and eye shadow to make them more noticeable.

He seemed a little surprised to see her as he shifted his attention away from Tony and Bill. "Oh, hi, Melanie. How's it going?"

"Super." Frantically she tried to think of a compliment. "That's a really great-looking shirt you're wearing. I just love solid colors."

As soon as she said that, she felt foolish, Nobody *loved* solid colors. It had sounded dumb, but Scott was smiling anyway, as if he thought she had wonderful taste. Flirting was working for a second time! And the idea made her totally ecstatic.

THE FABULOUS FIVE

The Trouble With Flirting

Betsy Haynes

A BANTAM SKYLARK BOOK®
TORONTO · NEW YORK · LONDON · SYDNEY · AUCKLAND

RL 5, 009–012
THE TROUBLE WITH FLIRTING
A Bantam Skylark Book / October 1988

Skylark Books is a registered trademark of Bantam Books, a
division of Bantam Doubleday Dell Publishing Group, Inc.
Registered in U.S. Patent and Trademark Office and elsewhere.

ISBN 0-553-15633-0

Published simultaneously in the United States and Canada

Bantam Books are published by Bantam Books, a division of Bantam Doubleday Dell Publishing Group,
Inc. Its trademark, consisting of the words "Bantam Books" and the portrayal of a rooster, is Registered in
U.S. Patent and Trademark Office and in other countries. Marca Registrada. Bantam Books, 666 Fifth
Avenue, New York, New York 10103.

PRINTED IN THE UNITED STATES OF AMERICA

0 9 8 7 6 5 4 3 2

CW

The Trouble With
Flirting

CHAPTER

1

"*I* am not boy crazy!" Melanie Edwards insisted. A hurt expression crossed her face as she sank back into the booth at Bumpers, the fast food restaurant that was the junior high hangout, and scanned her four best friends' faces for signs of sympathy.

"Hey, look," said Katie Shannon. "Here comes Scott Daly, and he's with Shane Arrington. What do you suppose they're talking about?"

Melanie's eyes brightened and she spun around, looking hopefully toward the front door where kids were streaming in for after-school sodas. Her shoulders slumped the instant she realized that Katie had only been teasing her, pretending that the two boys

1

she had mad crushes on were coming into Bumpers together.

Katie was laughing, and so were Jana Morgan, Beth Barry, and Christie Winchell, the other members of The Fabulous Five. The five of them had been best friends for practically forever and had made a pact to stick together when they left Mark Twain Elementary for Wakeman Junior High, or Wacko Junior High, as most kids called it. Melanie laughed too, in spite of herself. She knew her friends loved to tease her about her interest in boys. But how could she help it? There were so many more cute guys in junior high than there had been in her old elementary school.

"Listen, you guys," she said. "I just happen to like boys, that's all. What's so unusual about that?"

Jana leaned toward Melanie, her smile fading. "Speaking of boys, have you heard any more about Laura McCall's party?"

Melanie frowned. Laura McCall was the leader of The Fantastic Foursome, a clique of seventh-grade girls who had gone to Riverfield Elementary School together before coming to Wakeman. They had already established themselves as major rivals of The Fabulous Five. According to what Melanie and her friends had heard, Laura lived with her divorced father and could do absolutely anything she wanted to. What was even worse, there was a rumor out that she was having a party, and had invited lots of kids from her old school and ALL the boys from The Fabulous Five's school but NONE OF THE GIRLS. Melanie and her friends were burned up about that. It was obvious to them that Laura and her friends were trying to steal their boyfriends.

"No," said Melanie, shaking her head. "All I know is that Lisa Snow found out from Mark Peters that Laura and The Fantastic Foursome are passing out invitations in *red envelopes*, and that every single seventh-grade boy from Mark Twain Elementary got one—including Scott Daly. And even worse, according to Mark, they're all planning to go!"

"What a dirty trick," said Christie.

"It just means that Laura's afraid of the competition," Katie said smugly.

"Yeah," agreed Beth. "She knows that if The Fabulous Five were there, she'd never stand a chance."

Melanie didn't answer. She was too worried. Everyone knew that Laura had a crush on Shane Arrington, the gorgeous guy from her old school, and that she had had parties before just so she could invite him. Shane could win a River Phoenix look-alike contest hands down, but there were other things about him that were special, too. He had parents who were hippies and a pet iguana named Igor. For Laura to go after Shane was bad enough, now that Melanie liked him, too, in addition to still liking her old boyfriend, Scott Daly. But for Laura to invite the Mark Twain boys to this party meant that she would have the perfect opportunity to go after *both* Shane and Scott at once without any interference from The Fabulous Five. The idea made Melanie's reddish-brown hair curl.

"I can't believe that Randy Kirwan will go," Jana said in a sad voice. "Not after all we've meant to each other."

Beth nodded. "Or Keith Masterson, either."

"Well, if Scott goes, Laura had better keep her hands off him," Melanie said indignantly.

"So, what are you going to do if she doesn't?" asked Katie.

"I don't know, but I'll think of something."

Just then Marcie Bee squeezed through the crowd around the counter and headed for their booth. "Hi, gang," she chirped. "Did you see who just came in?" She nodded in the direction of a tall, sandy-haired boy who was making his way among the tables and heading in the general direction of The Fabulous Five. "*That's* Garrett Boldt," said Marcie. "Isn't he cute!"

"He's not just cute," said Melanie. She grabbed the table for support as her eyes lit up. "He's absolutely gorgeous!"

Just then Marcie shouted, "Hey, Garrett!"

Melanie's eyes widened. How could Marcie make such an idiot of herself? Melanie thought for an instant that she would die if she couldn't crawl away somewhere and hide. Maybe she could slip under the table before it was too late.

Garrett stopped and looked slowly in the direction of the booth where Marcie had slid in next to The Fabulous Five. Then a smile broke across his face. It wasn't an ordinary smile, though, Melanie thought. In fact, it was such an *extra*ordinary smile that her heart began to pound like crazy. His blue eyes sparkled and his mouth tilted higher on the left side than the right, emphasizing a deep dimple in his left cheek that appeared the instant he smiled.

"Hi, Marcie. How's it going?" he called back in a husky voice. Then, before Melanie had time to recover from the sight of his great smile and the sound of his romantic voice, he started toward the booth.

"Garrett's an eighth-grader and he's in my French class," Marcie whispered, trying to say the words without moving her lips so that Garrett wouldn't know she was talking about him. "He borrowed a pencil from me—*twice*." Beaming with pride and looking straight at him, she said out loud, "Wow! That's a neat camera."

For the first time Melanie pulled her eyes away from his face and noticed the camera hanging from a wide strap on his shoulder. It looked a lot like her father's expensive 35 mm.

"You probably won't see much of me without this baby," Garrett said, patting the camera. "I'm the sports photographer for the yearbook this year, and my job is to get pictures of all the jocks—in and out of the games."

Even though Garrett was answering Marcie's question, he was smiling and glancing around at all of the girls sitting in the booth as if each one of them was part of the conversation. "That reminds me, the soap game is Saturday afternoon. You girls are going, aren't you?"

Melanie felt limp. From the way he had asked, he made it sound as if he really wanted all of them at the game.

"What in the world is a soap game?" asked Katie, and Melanie realized that she had never heard of it either. "Is there some kind of new sport called soap?"

Garrett chuckled and then turned his gorgeous blue eyes on Katie. "It's a Wakeman tradition, and it's the first football game of the year except it doesn't count as part of the season. Actually, it's a preseason scrimmage between the first- and second-string players, and the price of admission is a bar of soap."

"A bar of soap!" shrieked Beth. "You've got to be kidding."

Garrett shook his head. "Honest," he said, and then raised his right hand as if he were swearing an oath. "The soap collected at the gate will be enough for the team's showers for the entire season. It's a terrific idea. So, are you going?"

"Of course we're going," said Melanie. "We wouldn't miss it for the world."

Garrett gave the girls a friendly wave as he turned and moved among the booths and tables, stopping here and there to speak to friends. Marcie drifted to another table, too, and for a moment The Fabulous Five just sat there, watching him walk away without uttering a word. They couldn't. They were speechless.

"Wow!" said Melanie after a minute. "Did you hear that? He wants us to go to the game."

Katie frowned at Melanie. "But why did you tell him we were going? We haven't even talked about it yet."

"Are you kidding?" said Melanie. "I'd *kill* to get to that game! I'd walk barefoot over burning coals! I'd dig my way through an avalanche! I'd bring a case of soap! I'd—"

"We get it! We get it!" shouted Christie. Then in a softer voice she added, "But I'll have to admit, it would take a lot to keep me away."

"Me, too," admitted Beth.

Katie was shaking her head in disbelief. "I don't know about you, Melanie," she said. "First it was Shane Arrington, and now it's Garrett Boldt. What about Scott Daly? In sixth grade, he was all you ever talked about. You haven't totally forgotten about him already, have you?"

"Of course not," Melanie insisted, but deep inside, underneath her excitement at going to the soap game on Saturday and seeing Garrett Boldt again, was a tiny stab of guilt over Scott.

CHAPTER

2

*M*elanie was ecstatic. *Everyone* was going to the soap game. From the moment it was first announced the next day during homeroom, right up until time to go to the stadium on Saturday afternoon, the game was the hot topic of conversation at school.

"I'm so *nervous*," Melanie confessed the minute she and the rest of The Fabulous Five met on the corner two blocks from the stadium to walk together to the game. "Scott and Shane are both on the team, and Garrett will be there taking pictures."

"I'm nervous, too," said Jana. "Randy is going to be playing, and I keep remembering the game last year when he got hurt."

9

"It was only a bloody nose," said Christie.

"I know," said Jana, "but it makes me nervous, anyway. Besides that, I want to look over the varsity cheerleaders. Seventh-graders get to try out next week for the junior varsity squad. I've got my fingers crossed that they won't have a lot of acrobatics in their routines. Otherwise, I'm *doomed*."

"Look," said Katie as they approached the entrance to the stadium. "Over there." Her voice had an ominous sound to it, and they looked quickly in the direction she was pointing.

"The Fantastic Foursome," muttered Christie. "Wouldn't you know they'd be here."

Melanie gave them a suspicious glance, but if Laura McCall and her three best friends noticed The Fabulous Five, they didn't let on. They were standing near the gate talking among themselves. Laura was obviously in control. She was taller than the rest and wore her hair in a long blond braid that fell from the top of her head to her waist. Standing in a semicircle around her were tiny, dark-haired Tammy Lucero, Melissa McConnell, who looked very serious, and bouncy, smily Funny Hawthorne.

"I'll bet Laura is giving them instructions," said Beth.

"I wonder what she makes them do to stay in her group," said Melanie. There was a big rumor around school that Laura gave her followers orders and that they obeyed them or else they were *out*, but so far nobody could find out what those orders were.

"She's probably telling them to scout the soap game for more cute boys to ask to her party," Katie said sarcastically.

"Oh, no!" cried Melanie. "What if she asks Garrett, too? Then she'll have Scott and Shane and Garrett—*all three*—in her clutches. I'll absolutely die!"

"Come on," urged Jana. "Let's go on in and find a seat before it gets too crowded."

The girls handed bars of soap to the ticket takers, who dropped them into large cardboard boxes. Then they entered the crowded stadium grounds.

"Want to go to the refreshment stand before we sit down?" shouted Melanie over the noise of the crowd. "I'm starved."

"No way!" said Beth. "Look at the stands. They're packed. If we don't find a seat right now, we may have to stand up through the whole game."

"Do you see anybody we know?" asked Jana, scanning the bleachers.

"That looks like Alexis Duvall and Lisa Snow and Kim Baxter over there," said Christie. She was pointing to the far section of the bleachers where most of the parents sat.

"Look this way," shouted Melanie. "Marcie Bee is over here with Gloria Drexler, and there are some empty seats behind them. If we hurry, we can get them."

Marcie and Gloria were sitting in the middle of the cheering section directly behind the team bench, and they saw The Fabulous Five, too, and began waving. It wasn't until they were already racing up the steps toward the empty seats that Melanie realized they weren't the only ones heading toward them. Climbing the steps on the opposite side of the section was The Fabulous Five's old enemy, Taffy Sinclair, followed by Stacy Holgrem and Sara Sawyer. Taffy was moving fast, and even though she was acting prissy and taking dainty little steps, Melanie could see that she was going to get there ahead of them.

"Come on, Edwards. Go for it!" urged Beth.

Melanie nodded and started taking the steps two at a time. When she and Taffy both reached the row, Melanie went crashing in from her side, crunching the toes of the people already seated and practically falling into the first empty space. Then she scooted toward the center, determined either to beat Taffy or squeeze her out.

"Oh, no, you don't, Melanie Edwards!" Taffy shouted. She made an unladylike dive for the space next to Melanie and came up with her nose practically touching Melanie's.

"I got here first," Melanie growled. "Go find someplace else to sit."

"Make me!" Taffy challenged. "Come on, kids," she said, motioning to Stacy and Sara. "These are our seats."

At the same time, Melanie motioned to her friends, who were stomping into the row and crowding themselves into the remaining space beside her. Beth wiggled in and Christie pressed herself in beside them. On the other side of Taffy, Stacy and Sara were struggling to wedge themselves into a space hardly big enough for one.

"Shove Taffy over," ordered Katie as she tried to cram herself into the shrinking space. "We need more room."

Glaring at Taffy, Melanie planted her bottom firmly on the hard bench of the bleachers and tried to inch her over. Taffy had planted her bottom on the bench, also, and was trying to do the same thing to Melanie while she gave her a terrible poison-dart look.

"I said move, and I meant it," snarled Melanie. "These seats belong to us. We got here first."

"It's a free country," Taffy said in a voice loud enough to be heard all around them. "We can sit here if we want to. Besides," she said, "isn't that Scott Daly over on the sidelines motioning to you?"

"What!" Melanie shrieked, jumping to her feet. The instant Melanie was off the bench, Taffy scooted over into her place.

"Oh, no, you don't," Melanie muttered when she realized she had been tricked. Then she sat down again as hard as she could, practically squashing Taffy. Melanie stared her straight in the eye as she shouldered into her space again. It took ages to wiggle her way back down to the bench, but she did it without pulling her eyes away from Taffy's for an instant.

Suddenly the horn bleated, signaling the start of the game and startling Melanie so much that she jumped as if she had hiccups. Had the cheerleaders already been out on the field? She had wanted to watch them since she planned to try out for the junior varsity squad, too.

The crowd roared as the center snapped the ball, and the two facing teams plowed headlong into each other. Melanie couldn't believe that both teams had gone through their warm-up calisthenics and the game had already started, and she was just now paying attention. She scanned the players on the field to see if she could spot either Scott or Shane. She found them immediately in their uniforms of red and gold, which were the Wakeman school colors. Scott was number 27 and Shane was number 31, and they were both on the second-string team, which was made up mostly of seventh-graders.

Suddenly movement on the sidelines directly below caught Melanie's attention. Her heart almost stopped. It was Garrett Boldt. He had turned to face the crowd, and there was a smile on his gorgeous face. Best of all, he had his camera in one hand, and with the other he was waving like crazy straight in her direction.

Melanie took a deep breath, smiling her most alluring smile and returning his wave. But suddenly she was aware of something going on beside her. Turning toward Taffy, Melanie saw that her old enemy was smiling so big that she could see her one crooked bicuspid, and that Taffy was waving at Garrett, too.

Self-consciously Melanie lowered her hand. How could she have ever thought that Garrett was waving to her? she wondered. Not with Taffy Sinclair around. Taffy not only had long blond hair and big blue eyes, but she had been the most gorgeous girl in Mark Twain Elementary. There weren't very many girls in Wakeman who were even close to being as pretty as she was.

But on the other hand, she reminded herself, Garrett had stopped by the booth at Bumpers where she had been sitting with the rest of The Fabulous Five, and he had smiled and acted as if he really wanted all of them, including her, to come to the soap game. But had he actually been flirting as she had hoped, or did he simply have a great personality and was friendly to everyone?

Melanie and Taffy glared at each other and continued elbowing for more room until Melanie suddenly realized that the entire first half was over and the cheerleaders were on the field. She had missed the whole thing. She had even missed hearing Christie's asking if anyone wanted anything from the refreshment stand. Now she noticed her friend struggling to get into the crowded row without spilling any of the goodies she was carrying.

"Melanie, I've got to talk to you," Christie called in a loud whisper. Her voice sounded urgent, as if she knew some big secret.

Melanie glanced over her shoulder at Taffy, knowing she didn't dare move from her spot. Taffy would be sure to crowd her out permanently if she got up even for a minute.

"What is it?" Melanie asked. "Can't you come down here and tell me?"

Christie sighed loudly as if she were totally exasperated, but a moment later she was leaning across Beth and cupping her hands around Melanie's ear.

"It's about Garrett Boldt," she whispered. "He was at the refreshment stand when I was, and guess what?"

"Come on, Christie," Melanie whined impatiently. *"Tell me!"*

"He asked me for your name and phone number!"

Melanie's eyes widened in disbelief and she thought for an instant that she might pass out from sheer excitement. Garrett had asked for her name and phone number? Not Taffy Sinclair's? It was too wonderful to be true.

"You're kidding!" she shrieked. "Oh, Christie. You're the best friend in the world!"

Melanie settled back and tried to concentrate on the rest of the game, but she couldn't. She was remembering how she had been overweight for so long from constantly eating her mother's scrumptious homemade brownies. She hadn't been *just* overweight, she remembered with a blush. She hadn't paid much attention to her hair or clothes, telling herself that her appearance didn't really matter, when, of course, it did. It hurt to remember how no boy had ever looked at her the way they looked at other girls, especially Taffy Sinclair. If they noticed her at all, they treated her like a sister.

But in sixth grade something wonderful had happened. She had started losing weight and wearing nicer clothes and even styling her hair, the way the other girls did. Finally Scott Daly had asked her to go to a movie with him and a bunch of other kids. She liked Scott a lot. And yet, there were tons of other cute boys in Wacko Junior High whom she hadn't even met yet.

So what if Katie Shannon is always calling me boy crazy? she thought. It didn't matter. Because now, even when she was sitting next to Taffy Sinclair, someone as special as Garrett Boldt had noticed *her*.

CHAPTER

3

After the soap game Bumpers was packed with kids from Wacko Junior High. Melanie loved the way the place was decorated with brightly painted bumper cars that were relics of an old amusement-park ride. The Fabulous Five had gotten there early enough to get one of the big booths. It was in a perfect location, near enough to the door to see everybody who came in, but close to the counter where kids put in their food and drink orders, too.

As Melanie scanned the room, she realized that most of the kids who had crowded into Bumpers so far were girls. One table was filled with eighth- and ninth-grade cheerleaders. Melanie gazed longingly

18

at them in their short, red, pleated skirts and gold letter sweaters. She wanted more than anything to make the seventh-grade squad. The football players were probably still in the showers using the bars of soap contributed at the game. They would be here in a little while, though. It was part of the Wakeman football tradition that everybody gathered at Bumpers after a game.

"I wish Garrett would hurry and get here," Melanie said in a dreamy voice. He had been the only thing she could think about ever since Christie told her that he had asked for her name and phone number, and Melanie was keeping one eye on the door so that she would know when he arrived. "I wonder where he is?"

"Didn't he say he has to get pictures of all the jocks for the yearbook?" asked Christie.

"Yeah," said Katie. "Maybe he's in the locker room photographing them in their underwear."

Everybody giggled at that.

"Don't you just love football players?" said Beth. "Did you see Keith block that pass? He's such a great player."

"Randy, too," said Jana. "I don't care if the second-string team did lose. They were terrific."

Just then Garrett came through the door. As usual, his camera hung from his shoulder as he waved to some kids near the front and sauntered up to the order counter. Melanie watched closely as his food was placed on a tray. He was having a bacon cheeseburger, large fries, and a large Coke. Yum! she thought. That's exactly what I'll have, too.

Suddenly a cheer went up as the first group of players came in the door, water droplets still glistening in their hair. They were all seventh-graders formerly from Mark Twain Elementary. Randy Kirwan was in the lead, followed by Mark Peters, Scott Daly, Keith Masterson, Joel Murphy, Matt Zeboski, and Clarence Marshall. They were smiling broadly even though the first-string team had beaten them 28 to 0.

"Oh, look," cried Jana, bouncing up and down in her seat. "They're heading this way." She was waving wildly so that they couldn't help noticing.

"Jana, stop waving like that," Melanie scolded. "We don't have enough room for all of them."

"I know that, silly," Jana said. "I just want to make sure Randy knows where I'm sitting."

Melanie sank back against the booth. What was she going to do now? Of all the times for this to happen. Of course Randy would sit with Jana. And when that happened Keith would be sure to sit with Beth, and then Scott would sit with her. That's the way it had worked all the time at Mama Mia's when they were in sixth grade. She had loved it then because she really liked Scott. I still like Scott, she reminded herself. But that was before Shane and

Garrett had come into the picture and complicated things.

Matt Zeboski peeled off in the direction of Mona Vaughn's table, and Clarence Marshall, Mark Peters, and Joel Murphy stopped to order something to eat, but the other three were marching straight for the booth where The Fabulous Five sat. To Melanie each step closer they came was like one ominous tick of a time bomb.

"Don't any of you guys get it?" she blurted to her friends while the boys were still too far away to hear. "Garrett Boldt asked for my phone number, but do you think he'll still want to call me if he sees me sitting with someone else? The answer is *no*."

"Oh, Melanie," said Katie in an exasperated voice, "you are the most boy crazy person I know."

Melanie glared at her friend. Katie couldn't possibly understand how it felt to change from an ugly duckling to a swan because she had been thin all her life. Besides that, Katie hardly knew that boys existed. But before she could answer Katie, the three boys were standing beside their booth.

"Do you have room for us?" asked Keith, diving in beside Beth before anyone could reply. On the other side, Katie and Christie and Jana shifted to let Scott slide in beside Melanie and Randy sit beside Jana.

"How did you like the game?" Scott asked Melanie. "Did you see that great tackle I made in the third quarter?"

"Sure," she lied. "It was terrific." Melanie tried to smile at Scott and look around the restaurant at the same time. Where had Garret gone? And where was Shane? She hadn't spotted him at all yet. Had they seen Scott sit down with her?

Suddenly she saw Garrett heading back toward the order counter. Had he forgotten something? Ketchup for his fries, maybe? What if he saw her with Scott?

Instantly, Melanie dove under the table, banging her head on the edge. All she could think about was hiding so that Garrett wouldn't see her.

She heard Scott gasp, and then his face appeared sideways in the opening between the table and the seat. "What are you doing down there?" he asked incredulously. "Are you okay?"

Melanie grinned sheepishly. "I'm fine," she assured him. "I just dropped a quarter. I'll be up in a minute."

She waited as long as she dared and then squeezed back up beside Scott. Her head had begun to throb, and she could feel a little lump growing on it, but that didn't matter. She was safe. Garrett had left the order counter and was talking to two boys in a green bumper car, his back turned so that he was facing away from her.

"I'm going to get something to eat," said Scott. "Playing football makes me so hungry."

"Me, too," echoed Randy and Keith.

"Do you want me to bring you something?" asked Scott.

Melanie shook her head. Her appetite was suddenly gone. But just as the boys slid out of the booth, she realized how thirsty she was and handed Scott some money for a Coke. Leaning back, she watched him approach the order counter. He's really terrific, she thought. He's cute and a great football player and not at all clumsy like Curtis Trowbridge, who fell over his own feet at least once a day.

Just then she noticed Shane Arrington come into Bumpers with two boys she had seen around school. They were looking for some place to sit. As Shane's eyes swept the room, Melanie panicked. She couldn't let him see her—Scott would be back any minute. She ducked behind Katie and held her breath.

"What are you doing?" Katie snapped.

"Pipe down," whispered Melanie. "I'm not doing anything."

"Then why are you scrunched up behind me?" Katie had twisted around and was peering down at Melanie.

"If you must know, I don't want Shane Arrington to see me and realize that I'm with Scott. It might spoil my chances with Shane later. Will you lean forward a little bit? I know he can see me this way."

Katie groaned, but she moved forward. Melanie breathed a sigh of relief and leaned her head against the back of the booth. Handling three boys at once was exhausting. Slowly she inched up just enough so that only her eyes were above the back of the booth. It was time to check things out. Scott was still in line at the order counter, but it looked as if Shane and his friends were talking to The Fantastic Foursome. Melanie leaned as far as she could to the right, but a post was blocking her view. And where was Garrett? From where she was sitting she couldn't see him anywhere.

Sighing, she thought about how much she liked Scott. I really do, she insisted to herself. But still she couldn't resist the idea of someday having a date with Shane or Garrett. Or maybe all three. She closed her eyes and imagined herself reserving Friday nights for movies with Scott, and Saturday afternoons for ball games with Garrett, and Sunday afternoons for pizza with Shane. There's only one way to make it all happen, she thought with new determination.

"I'm going to the ladies' room," she announced, pushing her way out of the booth. It was the best excuse she could think of to get up and move around Bumpers. She could never make any progress with Shane or Garrett while pinned in a booth next to Scott Daly.

Melanie ducked into the ladies' room and ran her brush through her windblown hair. Then she added a little lip gloss and stood back from the mirror, surveying herself with satisfaction.

Luckily she was alone in the ladies' room, so she opened the door a crack and peeked out. Scott was not in the order line anymore, which meant he was probably back at the booth and wondering where she was. She could see Shane. He had moved away from Laura McCall and her friends and was talking to some guys. At least that much was going her way. But where was Garrett? She pushed the door open a little bit farther and looked for him again. No luck. Rats!

Melanie took a deep breath and silently rehearsed the list of rules for walking across a crowded room that she had learned in the modeling class she and the rest of The Fabulous Five had taken last year. Then she opened the door and stepped out.

Bumpers was crowded, all right, and noisy. Kids were laughing and shouting to each other, and over it all music blared from an antique Wurlitzer jukebox. Melanie smiled to herself as she began weaving through the tables and booths. She tried to act casual, stopping to say hello to Alexis Duvall and waving to Mona Vaughn and Matt Zeboski, but every second she was on the lookout for Garrett. As soon as she spotted him, she would simply walk up to his table, give him a dazzling smile, and then move on, leaving him love-struck as he gazed after her. It always worked in soap operas on TV.

But where was he? There wasn't an empty table in the place, but try as she might, she couldn't spot him sitting at any of them. Just then she looked toward the door. There he was, and his hand was on the knob. *Oh, no. He's leaving!* she wanted to shout, but instead she bit her lip. As she watched, he opened the door and walked out without even so much as looking back.

"*I blew it*," she grumbled to herself. "While I was hiding behind Katie and primping in the ladies' room, he was probably looking everywhere for me, and what did I do? I missed my big chance."

CHAPTER

4

*M*elanie went straight to her room when she got home from Bumpers, leaning back against plump pillows on her bed and opening her notebook to a clean sheet of paper. Then she began to write.

Melanie Edwards

+

Garrett Boldt

That looks nice, she thought. In fact, it looked terrific. Still, she couldn't forget Shane and Scott,

27

so she turned to another clean page and started again.

Melanie Edwards Melanie Edwards Melanie Edwards

        +   +   +

Shane Arrington   Garrett Boldt   Scott Daly

That looked even nicer. But which one did she really like the best? What a choice, she thought, shaking her head. Shane was *so* interesting. How many boys had she ever met before who had hippie parents and an iguana named Igor for a pet? None! And then there was Garrett. Wow! He was just about as gorgeous as one guy could get, and he was an eighth-grader. It was the first time someone older and more sophisticated had ever been interested in her, and it was fun.

But how could she ignore Scott Daly? She was so comfortable around him, and she had thought for a long time that they would probably get married someday. Melanie Daly, she wrote. That looked super. Melanie Elizabeth Daly. Melanie Elizabeth Edwards Daly. Or how about, Melanie Edwards-Daly?

Sighing, she closed her eyes and pictured how her name would look if she married Shane or Garrett. Melanie Arrington, she thought, or Melanie Boldt.

Through her closed door she could hear the distant ring of the phone. By the time her mother knocked softly on the door to say that the call was for her, she was already naming the children. Garrett Boldt, Jr. Or should it be Garrett Boldt, II?

She pulled herself out of her daydream and went to the phone. "Hello."

"Hi, Melanie. This is Garrett Boldt."

Melanie's hand started shaking and she almost dropped the phone. She would know that husky, romantic voice anywhere.

"Hi," she whispered, but then, remembering that she had already said hello, she felt herself blush.

"In case you're wondering, I got your phone number from a girl sitting near you in the bleachers. Did you go to Bumpers after the game?" he asked. "I looked around for you, but I couldn't find you anywhere."

"I was there," Melanie assured him. "And I saw you. Maybe I was in the ladies' room when you were looking for me." Then she felt another blush creep up her face and she added quickly, "Combing my hair."

"I got some great pictures at the game," he said. "I'll show them to you after I develop them if you're interested."

"I'd love to see them. Are you going to develop them yourself?"

"Sure. I have my own darkroom," he said proudly.

Melanie was so impressed that she didn't know what to say next. Finally Garrett spoke.

"Well, I'll definitely see you at school on Monday. You will be there, won't you?"

"You bet," said Melanie. "And I'll be sure to say hello."

After they said good-bye, Melanie hung up and then hugged herself with joy. He had been looking for her, after all. Wow, she thought. It's a good thing I didn't let him see me with Scott.

"Who was that, dear?" called her mother from the kitchen. "It didn't sound like Scott."

Melanie wandered into the kitchen and watched her mother lift hot chocolate chip cookies off a cookie sheet with a spatula and place them carefully on a plate. She always thought of her family as being old-fashioned. Her parents weren't divorced like so many kids' she knew, and her mother stayed home and took care of Melanie and her six-year-old brother, Jeffy, baking cookies and things like that.

"It wasn't Scott," she said as she picked up a cookie with two fingers and blew on it to cool it. "His name is Garrett Boldt, and he's an eighth-grader."

"An *eighth-grader?*" her mother echoed, raising one eyebrow to show her surprise. "Did you meet him at school?"

Melanie shook her head. "At Bumpers, and he asked Christie for my name and phone number at the game today."

She started to tell her mother the whole story, but just then the phone rang again. "I'll get it," she sang over her shoulder. Maybe it was Garrett calling again.

"Oh, Melanie. I've just got to talk to you."

It was Jana, and it sounded as if she was crying.

"What's the matter?" Melanie asked. "Are you okay?"

"Yes . . . no . . . Oh, I don't know," said Jana. "It's Randy. He got one of Laura's invitations in a red envelope, and he says he's going to her party, even though he knows I wasn't invited."

"You're kidding!" said Melanie. "I can't believe Randy Kirwan would do a thing like that."

"Neither could I, at first," said Jana. "I thought he was just joking. But when I asked him if he really planned to go, he said yes. He said all the guys were going just to see what one of Laura's parties is like, and they would tease him if he didn't go, too. Of course he tried to tell me that he wouldn't have any fun without me there, but I know he was only saying that to keep me from getting mad. But I'll tell you something else. It didn't work!"

Melanie sighed. She couldn't blame Jana for getting mad. "If Randy is going, then Scott is probably going, too."   •

"Of course he is," insisted Jana. "They all are. Scott. Keith. Randy. Every one of them. If Scott didn't tell you, it was probably because you didn't ask him about it. He wouldn't want to admit it if he didn't have to."

Melanie thought a moment. She had chattered all the way home from Bumpers, hardly giving Scott a chance to say anything. Partly she had done it because she was excited to have three gorgeous boys to like, and partly it was to cover up her guilty conscience over not wanting the other two to see her with Scott. But now that she knew for sure that he was going to Laura's party, she was as angry at him as Jana was at Randy.

"How dare those boys go to Laura McCall's party," Melanie said. "And if Scott Daly thinks he has me wrapped around his little finger and can get away with a thing like that, he has another thing coming. Besides," she added, and smiled to herself, "Garrett Boldt called me a few minutes ago, just the way Christie said he would. Maybe I'll go out with him. And if you want me to, I'll ask him if he has a friend for you."

"I don't want to go out with anyone but Randy," said Jana, and Melanie couldn't be sure, but she thought Jana was crying again.

After they hung up, Melanie thought the situation over. She liked Scott, but if he was going to do something as rotten as going to Laura McCall's party, she would just have to concentrate on the other boys in her life, Shane and Garrett. Shane was difficult. She only had biology class with him, and she had already asked him about his pet iguana, Igor. She would have to think of some way to get his attention.

And then there was Garrett. Gorgeous Garrett, she thought as she closed her eyes and pictured his handsome face with the big dimple that always appeared in his left cheek when he smiled. He wouldn't be much easier since he was an eighth-grader and didn't even have the same lunch period. She would have to depend on his phone calls, at least for now.

She picked up the new teen magazine that had come in the day's mail and sank onto her bed again. She was depressed from Jana's call about the boys' going to Laura's party, and she certainly didn't feel like writing her name plus the boys' names or picking names for the children anymore. She made a face at the smiling model on the magazine cover and turned to the table of contents. Reading quickly down the list of articles, she was jolted by the title of an article on page 49: "Seven Tips for Flirting" by Miriam Dunmore.

"Seven tips for flirting!" she whispered gleefully. "That's just what I need." She turned to page 49 and began skimming the article, not taking time to read the entire piece, but looking for the numbered tips and jotting them into her notebook.

"This is terrific," she said out loud as she began repeating the tips over and over to memorize them. "(1) Make eye contact with the boy you are flirting with; (2) Act happy and self-confident; (3) Use positive body language; (4) Give compliments; (5) Show genuine interest in him; (6) Ask him questions; and (7) Be a good listener."

Wow! she thought. That's all there is to flirting? This is a piece of cake. Look out, guys. Here I come.

By time for school Monday morning, Melanie had practiced the seven tips for flirting until she was sure could recite them in her sleep if she had to. Also, she had almost forgotten her anger at Scott over Laura McCall's party and was feeling ecstatic again over Garrett's phone call.

"You should hear his dreamy voice over the phone," she bragged to her friends as they waited in their special spot by the fence for the first bell to ring. She had spent at least half an hour on the phone with each one of them over the weekend talking about Garrett's call, but she couldn't resist bringing it up again. "And he said that he actually looked for me at Bumpers. *Thank goodness* he didn't catch me sitting with Scott."

"Do you think he'll ask you out?" asked Beth.

"Yeah," said Christie. "Maybe he was just being friendly."

"Oh course he'll ask me out," said Melanie. "I mean, a guy doesn't ask for your phone number just to call and say hello. He was probably just getting up his nerve."

"I think you're right," said Jana.

"*I* think you're boy crazy," snipped Katie. "You ought to get involved in something worthwhile for a change. School elections are coming up in a few weeks. Have you thought about running for an office?"

Melanie frowned at Katie instead of answering. She could never understand Katie's attitude. How could any girl be so *uninterested* in boys and so *interested* in boring things such as school elections? Besides, once she put her flirting tips into action and got results, Katie would see that she had been wrong.

Melanie looked around the school ground for someone else she knew. She was bursting to tell everybody about Garrett. She spotted Alexis talking to Sara and Kim near the gum tree. Its bark was polka-dotted with wads of gum stuck there by students when the bell rang every morning, and it was near the front door of the school.

"I'll see you guys later," she called as she hurried away from The Fabulous Five. "Hey, Alexis, Sara, Kim, guess what!"

"Who knows?" answered Kim.

"Whatever it is, it must be pretty terrific," said Alexis.

Melanie could hardly control the grin that was spreading across her face. "Do you know who Garrett Boldt is?"

"Sure," said Sara. "He's an eighth-grader, isn't he? The hunk with the dimple?"

"That's the one. Well, I met him at Bumpers last week after school. Then Saturday, at the soap game, he saw me in the stands and waved at me. Taffy Sinclair thought he was waving at her, and she made an idiot of herself waving back. Then later at the refreshment stand, he asked Christie for my name and phone number, and after the game, he called me."

"Wow!" said Alexis. "You are so-o-o-o lucky. I'd give anything if he would ask for my phone number. What did he say? Did he ask you out?"

"Not yet," said Melanie confidently. "But he will, and I can't wait to see the look on Taffy Sinclair's face when she sees us together. She was so sure that he was waving at her."

"Uh-oh," said Sara. "Look over there." She pointed toward the front gate of the school.

Melanie gasped. "Oh, no," she murmured. Garrett Boldt was standing there. He was smiling so broadly that she could see his dimple, and he was talking to *Taffy Sinclair*.

The bell finally rang, and the school ground emptied as students filed into Wacko Junior High. Melanie was glad. She couldn't stand to watch Taffy Sinclair flirting with Garrett. Everybody knew what a terrible flirt Taffy was, of course, but that didn't help much. Neither did the memory of Taffy's waving at Garrett during the soap game. It was pretty clear that Taffy was after him, too.

CHAPTER

5

*M*elanie struggled to pay attention in her morning classes, but her thoughts kept focusing on her boy troubles instead. What was she going to do? She kept seeing pictures in her mind of Taffy Sinclair flirting with Garrett. There was only one thing to do. *Flirt*. If Taffy could do it, now she could do it better.

She got her first chance during lunch period. Stepping into the cold-drink line, she was amazed to see Shane Arrington standing just in front of her. She took a deep breath and mentally ran down the list of seven tips for flirting that she had read in the magazine. 1. Make eye contact. 2. Be self-confident and friendly. 3. Use positive body language. 4. Give compliments. But Melanie never got to number five, because just as she was wondering how she could possibly get up enough nerve to pay a compliment to Shane, he turned around and looked at her.

"HI!" she said, gazing straight into his eyes and giving him her best smile. She couldn't help worrying that her voice had been too loud or her eyes were bugged out, but it was too late now. She was into it, and she had to keep going. "That's really a great-looking shirt you're wearing. I just love plaid."

"You do?" Shane asked, and then he smiled so big that Melanie felt certain he couldn't have been more pleased if she had announced that she loved *iguanas*.

Her mind was whirling. *Use positive body language.* Stepping closer to him, she put a hand on his arm just the way the girl in the magazine picture had done and said, "Doesn't the hot lunch smell gross? I always bring a sandwich from home. I think they must use ground-up lizard in their meatloaf." Melanie gasped, suddenly realizing what she had just said. "I didn't mean iguanas," she sputtered. "Honest! I meant things like crocodiles and alligators. They're lizards, aren't they?"

Shane was laughing and nodding his head at the same time. "Actually, alligator meat is supposed to be pretty tasty. You can get it in restaurants in places like Florida and New Orleans. It's stuff made out of iguana that you have to watch out for. YUK!" Then his face got serious and he added, "You don't have an iguana sandwich in that lunch bag, do you?"

"Nope. Just plain old peanut butter and jelly." She tried to match his serious expression, which she knew was fake, but her mouth kept slipping into a grin.

By now the line had moved forward, and Shane was paying for his milk. As he started to walk away, he turned and smiled at her again. "Your name is Melody, isn't it?"

"Melanie," she corrected. "You were close."

"Okay, Melanie. See you later."

It had worked! She wanted to jump up and down and shout the good news to everyone in the cafeteria, but of course, she didn't. Instead she bought a carton of chocolate milk and drifted over to the table where the rest of The Fabulous Five had already gathered and sat down, feeling too dreamy and romantic to eat.

"What's the matter with you?" asked Katie.

"I just had a super conversation with Shane Arrington," she said. "All about crocodiles, alligator meat, and iguanas."

"Sounds divine," said Beth, crossing her eyes and making a silly face.

"You would have to have been there to understand," Melanie sniffed. Then breaking into a grin, she said, "I actually flirted with him and he flirted back."

Melanie scanned the crowded cafeteria, trying to catch sight of Scott. She was on a roll now, and she didn't want to stop. Even though she was still semi-angry with him. Unfortunately, she would have to wait to flirt with Garrett because he ate lunch next period with the eighth-graders.

She finally found Scott at the end of the hot-lunch line. He was talking to Tony Sanchez and Bill Soliday, two seventh-grade football players who had gone to Copper Beach Elementary. Not only that, but Laura McCall and Tammy Lucero were only a little way ahead of him in line, and both girls kept turning around and looking at the boys. That could spell trouble, Melanie thought. Gulping down her chocolate milk and stuffing her unopened lunch bag under her bulky sweater, she jumped to her feet.

"Anybody for hot lunch besides me?" she asked.

Her friends looked up at her in amazement.

"Are you kidding?" said Jana, waving a half-eaten cream cheese and jelly sandwich in the air. "We never buy hot lunch."

"I thought you brought your lunch today, too," said Christie.

"I did," Melanie confessed, "but I suddenly have a mad craving for mystery meat. See you guys in a few minutes." Tossing them a smile, she hurried to get in line behind Scott and silently rehearsed the tips for flirting as she went.

"Hi, Scott," she said sweetly. She opened her eyes wide and looked directly into his, wishing that she was wearing mascara and eye shadow to make them more noticeable.

He seemed a little surprised to see her as he shifted his attention away from Tony and Bill. "Oh, hi, Melanie. How's it going?"

"Super." Frantically she tried to think of a compliment. "That's really a great-looking shirt you're wearing. I just love solid colors."

As soon as she said that, she felt foolish. Nobody *loved* solid colors. It had sounded dumb, but Scott was smiling anyway, as if he thought she had wonderful taste. Flirting was working for a second time! The idea made her ecstatic.

The end of the hot-lunch line had reached the steam tables, and Scott was loading his tray with a giant submarine sandwich, fries, chocolate cake, and milk. She grabbed a tray and skimmed it along beside his, aware that Laura and Tammy were trying to hear what they were saying. It was time to try flirting tip #3, use positive body language. She leaned toward Scott and rested her hand gently on his arm. "I was so impressed with that great tackle you made in the soap game that I've been telling *everybody* about it."

It wasn't quite the truth, but Scott beamed at her so brightly that she forgot about feeling guilty.

"Really?" he asked. "I didn't think you liked football that much."

"It depends on who is playing," she said coyly.

Scott was still smiling at her, and she could feel Laura's and Tammy's eyes boring holes into her. This was a double whammy—flirting with Scott and making Laura and Tammy jealous.

Laura and Tammy paid for their lunches and stomped off to find a table, sticking their noses in the air to let her know how they felt about her flirting with Scott. He followed Tony and Bill away from the cashier, leaving Melanie to gaze after him and feel triumphant. This is almost too easy, she thought with a giggle.

"So, what's the big idea? Are you eating, or what?" The lady behind the cash register was glaring at her, and it took a few seconds for her to realize why. She had gone the whole length of the steam tables without putting a single thing on her tray.

Melanie fought down a wave of embarrassment. How could she have forgotten to get any food? Glancing around quickly, she saw that Laura and Tammy were on the other side of the lunchroom and Scott had his back turned. She was safe.

"Not today," she said, flashing a bright smile. Then she reached under her sweater and pulled out her lunch bag, plopping it down on the empty tray. "I brought my lunch." She tilted her chin triumphantly, and then she picked up her tray and went gliding across the cafeteria toward her friends, leaving the puzzled cashier staring after her.

CHAPTER

6

*A*fter school Melanie joined the crowd of girls shuffling into the gymnasium for the first meeting of seventh-graders who were interested in trying out for cheerleader. She looked around, just in case Jana or Beth had beaten her to the gym and saved her a seat, but they hadn't. The sight of so many girls competing for the eight positions on the seventh-grade squad made her more nervous than ever. Taffy Sinclair had managed to get a seat in the center of the front row, and beside her were Alexis Duvall and Sara Sawyer. In the second row Laura McCall twirled her long, blond braid and listened to Tammy Lucero, who was busily pointing out other girls in

44

the bleachers and whispering to her. They were gos-
siping again, Melanie thought indignantly. A few
rows higher Mandy McDermott waved when
Melanie looked her way. Mandy had gone to Copper
Beach Elementary and had been in the modeling
class with her that was held at Tanninger's Depart-
ment Store last spring. There were dozens of other
girls sprinkled across the bleachers. Some she knew,
but most she didn't.

She sat down in the fourth row and spread books
on either side to save seats for her friends, thinking
about how badly she wanted to be a Wakeman
cheerleader. Over and over again she had lain in bed
at night, gazing into the darkness and imagining herself in one of those darling little red pleated skirts
and matching gold letter sweaters jumping around in
front of a cheering crowd and waving her pom-
poms. And now, she realized, cheerleading would
also put her near the three boys of her dreams. She
could see it all. Garrett on the sidelines taking pictures for the yearbook and maybe even getting her
into a shot or two, and Scott and Shane on the field
of battle, inspired to victory by her enthusiasm and
by the excitement she and the other cheerleaders
could whip up among the fans. She had to make the
squad, she thought. She simply *had to*.

A moment later Beth stumbled breathlessly
through the row and sank down beside her. It was
obvious she had been hurrying. "I waited around at

Jana's locker for ages before I remembered that she won't make this first cheerleader meeting. The yearbook has its first meeting today, too, and she and Funny Hawthorne are applying for seventh-grade coeditors."

Melanie nodded. She had forgotten, also. She started to ask Beth if she thought Miss Wolfe would count the absence against Jana in competition when the gym teacher strode into the room and held up her hand for silence. Gitta Wolfe was tall and slim with hair the color of ripe wheat and with a fun-loving personality. She had moved to America from her native Germany as a child and pronounced both her own last name and the name of the school as if they began with *V*'s instead of *W*'s. What's more, she didn't seem to mind the occasional giggles that her mispronunciation inspired.

"Good afternoon, ladies," she said with a smile. "As you know, I am Miss Volfe, and I vill be coaching the seventh-grade cheerleading squad. At today's meeting I vill explain the categories you'll be judged on, and also the Vakeman varsity cheerleaders vill demonstrate some of the cheers and the gymnastic moves that you'll be required to do as members of the squad. Before you leave, you'll each get a set of mimeographed sheets containing the cheers so that you may study and practice them before tryouts on Friday. Any questions?"

Melanie was too awed to ask questions, and so, apparently, were all of the others since no hands went up.

"Then, good luck to each of you."

For the next hour they watched as the experienced eighth- and ninth-graders went through intricate routines full of finger snaps, foot motions, claps, straddle jumps, cartwheels, walk overs, splits, and pyramids, and all without missing a beat or garbling a word of the cheers.

"Impossible," said Beth as they collected their mimeographed sheets and filed out of the gym. "We've got to learn all that plus concentrate on the judging points: pep, execution of routines, personality, eye contact, personal appearance. What does she think we are, anyway?"

"Don't forget recovery from mistakes on the list of judging points," said Melanie. "That's going to be the biggie as far as I'm concerned. I can tell already."

Grinning, Beth pulled herself up to her full height and said in her best imitation of Miss Wolfe, "If you vant to be a cheerleader for Vacko Junior High, you *vill* recover from your mistakes!"

Both girls broke up laughing as they made their way down the hall, and Melanie couldn't help thinking that although she had lots of hard work ahead to make the squad, one thing was certain: with Beth around, it was going to be fun.

After supper she was in the living room going over the cheers on her sheets and self-consciously practicing the motions in front of Jeffy when the phone rang. "I get it! I get it!" Jeffy screamed as he dove to answer it. Melanie glared at him, thinking what a pest he was, as he put the receiver to his ear and announced proudly, "Edwards residence. This is Jeffy." Slowly his smile drizzled away as he listened. "Okay," he said dejectedly, and thrust the phone toward her. "It's a boy."

Melanie brightened. "Hello."

"Hi, Melanie, this is Garrett."

Of course it is, she thought as the sound of his husky voice turned her knees to mush. Backing up to the wall and sliding slowly down to a sitting position on the floor, she said, "So, how's the world's greatest sports photographer?"

"If you really want to know, not so great," he said. "Only about half of the pictures I took at the soap game turned out. Can you believe I was shooting at the wrong shutter speed? I don't know what I was thinking about when I did that."

ME! Melanie wanted to shout. *You were so dazzled when you saw me in the crowd that you couldn't think straight anymore.* But instead she said, "Gee. That's too bad."

"That wasn't what I really called about, though," Garrett assured her. "I just wondered how the cheerleader meeting went."

Melanie's jaw dropped almost to the floor. "How did you know that I went to the cheerleader meeting?"

"I saw you in the hall afterwards. Remember? I waved, and you waved back."

"Oh, yeah," Melanie said softly. When had she seen Garrett? She racked her brain. Had she been clowning around with Beth and missed seeing him? Had she been acting so goofy that he thought she was waving?

"So, aren't you going to tell me about the meeting?"

Melanie laughed nervously. "Sure. It was fun and interesting and definitely scary. I think at least half of the girls in seventh grade are trying out, and there are only eight spots on the squad."

"You'll do great," said Garrett, sending her heart soaring. "You probably know all the cheers already."

"As a matter of fact, I was practicing when you called."

"I'll let you go in a minute, then, so you can get back to your practicing. But first, there's one more thing I wanted to ask you."

This time, Melanie's heart burst through the ceiling. This was it! He was going to ask her out.

"I was wondering if you're going to Laura's party Saturday night?"

His words shot through her like an electric current. She was too much in shock to answer at first.

Finally she swallowed hard and said softly, "Sorry. I'm not invited."

"You're kidding. Why not?"

"Because I'm a girl and because I went to Mark Twain. Laura invited all of the boys from Mark Twain but none of the girls." Melanie tried not to sound catty, but she knew she did, anyway. "I guess she's afraid of the competition."

Garrett laughed softly. "Sounds like Laura. Listen, I know her pretty well. I went to Riverfield. I'll just remind her that's she's missing a great chance to show off. Believe me, there's almost nothing she likes better than showing off. I'll bet you'll get an invitation tomorrow."

"Not just me!" Melanie shrieked. Then regaining her composure, she added, "What I mean is, I'd feel self-conscious if I hardly knew any of the other girls."

"Okay," said Garrett. "I'll convince her to show off to *all* the Mark Twain girls."

After they had hung up Melanie sat on the floor for ages, dangling the phone from one hand. One minute she was thrilled over Garrett's wanting her to be at Laura's party. And the next she was in a total panic over actually going. What on earth am I getting myself into? she wondered over and over again.

CHAPTER

7

*F*our phone calls later, Melanie felt a little bit better—but only a little bit. She had talked to each of the other members of The Fabulous Five and told them about her conversation with Garrett and his promise to talk Laura McCall into inviting them to her party.

"Fantastic!" Jana had said. "With me there, Laura wouldn't dare try to steal Randy."

Beth had reacted pretty much the same way. "Terrific, Edwards!" she had shouted into the phone, practically breaking Melanie's eardrum. "She won't be able to get her clutches on Keith now."

Christie's reaction had been quieter, but enthusiastic just the same. "Gee, imagine *us* at one of Laura McCall's famous parties."

Even Katie had been mildly excited about going. "It will be interesting to see what Laura does at her own party." Then, after pausing for a moment, she added, "But what are you going to do, Melanie?"

"What do you mean?"

"Well," said Katie. "All three of the boys you like are going to be there."

"Oh, my gosh," Melanie mumbled just before she hung up. "I hadn't thought about that."

Now, back in her room with her French book propped open in front of her, she was certainly thinking about it. Hard. Seventh grade had started out like one of the fairy tales that she had always loved. Cinderella trying on the glass slipper and going to the ball with the handsome prince. Sleeping Beauty being awakened to a world of love by the prince of her dreams. Melanie Edwards adored by three handsome boys. Well, at least Scott adored her, and Shane and Garrett were coming around.

But now the wicked witch was trying to spoil everything by giving a party and inviting all three of them. She will probably invite me, too, Melanie thought, so that I can watch while she casts her spell on all of them.

Slamming her French book shut, Melanie jumped to her feet and paced her room. Maybe I shouldn't go, she thought. But that was out of the question. Of course she would go. She couldn't miss a thing such as that.

Melanie was nervous the next morning when she and her friends headed for their lockers. "What if Garrett wasn't able to convince Laura to invite us to her party?" she moaned. "Laura would feel so superior if she thought we wanted to go and all she had to do was say no. I'd die of embarrassment."

"Look! On my locker!" Beth cried.

Melanie blinked in disbelief as all five girls stopped and stared at Beth's locker, logjamming traffic in the hallway behind them for a moment. Stuck in the U-shaped shank of Beth's combination lock was a small red envelope—the same kind of envelope in which the boys had received invitations to Laura's party a few days before.

"Oh, my gosh," whispered Melanie. "He did it!"

As Beth grabbed the red envelope and tore it open, the other four girls raced to their own lockers. Melanie exhaled, releasing breath she didn't know she had been holding, and pulled the red envelope out of her lock, staring at it as if it might bite. Her hands were shaking so badly that she had trouble tearing it open, but there it was. Her own handwritten invitation to Laura McCall's party.

You're Invited to a Party

Where: 7034 Woodstock Drive, Apt. #7

When: Saturday night at 7 P.M.
Given by: Laura McCall

That was it. No bright little note in the corner
saying "Hope you can come!" No happy face drawn
beside Laura's name. Not the kind of invitation kids
usually sent. It was almost creepy. Melanie jammed
it into her pocket and got her books.

She was deep in thought and heading for her
homeroom when Taffy Sinclair and Sara Sawyer
came strutting up beside her. They were giggling
together as if they knew a big secret.

"You'll never guess what I found when I went to
my locker this morning," Taffy purred. She had a
catlike grin on her face, as if she couldn't be more
satisfied with herself.

"Don't tell me. Let me guess," Melanie grumbled.
"A red envelope."

Taffy gasped. "How did you know?"

"Because I got one, too. In fact, it's because of me
that you were even invited to Laura's party."

"I don't believe that!" Taffy huffed, and then exchanged knowing glances with Sara.

"Well, it's true. Garrett Boldt called me last night
and asked if I was going to Laura's party. I said no. I
told him that she hadn't invited any girls from Mark
Twain, and he said he would talk to Laura because
he wanted me to be there. Then," said Melanie,
glaring at Taffy through narrowed eyes, "I said that I

thought every girl from Mark Twain should be invited if I was. So there!"

Taffy raised her nose into the air, and Sara and she wheeled away. She couldn't have looked more surprised if I had said that school had just been canceled for the year, thought Melanie. She let a tiny giggle escape to keep a gigantic laugh from bursting out. It felt good to outdo Taffy Sinclair for a change.

For the rest of the morning whenever she saw any of the girls from Mark Twain, she told her story again, basking in their gratitude and enjoying the flickers of jealousy appearing on their faces at the mention of gorgeous Garrett Boldt.

Then, as she was changing classes between second and third periods, she saw Garrett. He had turned into the hall just ahead of her, and he was coming her way. Oh, my gosh! she thought as her free hand automatically brushed her hair. I wonder if I look okay.

He was walking along and staring straight ahead as if his mind were a million miles away.

"Hi, Garrett," she said shyly.

He stopped and glanced at her, but two or three seconds passed before recognition registered in his eyes. "Oh, hi," he said. "How's it going?"

"Great," said Melanie. She was surprised that he didn't seem particularly glad to see her. Maybe he gets shy around girls he likes, she reasoned. Aloud she said, "I found my invitation to Laura's party when I went to my locker before classes."

"Yeah? Well, it's going to be a great party. See you around." He gave her a casual wave and moved on down the hall. Boys! she thought, and shrugged helplessly. There was no way to understand them.

CHAPTER

8

*I*f Melanie had thought for one moment that Laura would invite The Fabulous Five to her party and let it go at that, she found out at lunchtime that she had been very much mistaken. She pushed the door open and went into the girls' room ahead of her friends and came face-to-face with Laura McCall and the rest of The Fantastic Foursome. They were all facing the door when Melanie walked in except Melissa McConnell, who was looking in the mirror and meticulously applying lip gloss with a tiny pink brush.

"Did you find the invitations to my party?" Laura asked.

There was a haughty sound in her voice that made Melanie feel as if she had been invited to an execution. "Yes, we did. Thanks."

"Well . . . are you coming or not?"

"We haven't decided yet," piped up Katie.

Melanie dug an elbow into Katie's ribs. "What Katie means is, we haven't had time to talk about it yet or check with our parents. We'll let you know as soon as we do."

"Gosh, I hope you guys come," said Funny. She and Jana had become friends during the first week of school, and now she was grinning at each of them. "Laura's parties are always super."

"'Super' isn't even the word for it," said Tammy. "They're fantastic! Ask anybody who's ever been to one."

"That's right," said Laura. She narrowed her eyes and smirked at them. "You'll be impressed right out of your socks. Ask *anybody*."

"We'll probably be there," Jana said quickly, and Melanie noticed that she was speaking mostly to Funny. "But we have to check it out at home first."

After The Fantastic Foursome left, Melanie and her friends clustered near the mirrors.

"The nerve of that girl!" said Melanie as she ran a brush through her reddish-brown hair.

"She really has us where she wants us, too," said Beth. "She knows we'd rather die than miss the party. Can you imagine how she's going to show off in front of us? I could throw up already just thinking about it."

"She's such a witch," said Jana. "I don't know why the others stay friends with her."

"Obviously they think it's a big deal to be known as her friends," said Katie. "Maybe we'll understand it better after we've been to her party and seen her in action."

"Action!" scoffed Melanie. "You know what that's going to be, don't you? She's going to steal our boyfriends right in front of our eyes."

Melanie was still fuming about Laura McCall as she stomped up the hall toward her first afternoon class. Rounding a corner, she almost smacked into Scott.

"Whoa!" he said, laughing and holding up his arms in mock surrender. "Where are you going so fast?"

Melanie grinned sheepishly. "Sorry. I didn't mean to mow you down. I guess I was concentrating on something so hard that I forgot to look where I was going."

"I know," he said confidently. "You were thinking about cheerleading tryouts. Hey, I just heard the good news."

"What good news?" asked Melanie, wondering if Miss Wolfe had already made a decision on the squad without her knowing about it.

"You're invited to Laura's party. That's terrific." Then leaning closer to her, he said confidentially, "I hear that her parties are terrific. I'm really glad you're going to be there."

Giving him her biggest smile, she said, "I wouldn't miss it for the world."

Melanie couldn't help feeling pleased as she moved on to class. First Garrett had gotten her the invitation, and now Scott was glad she was going. Two out of three wasn't bad, she told herself. Saturday night could turn out to be one of the most exciting nights of her life.

"Hi, Melody," someone called out behind her. Whirling around, she saw Shane Arrington hurrying to catch up with her.

"It's *Melanie*," she said, pretending to be hurt that he had gotten her name wrong again.

Shane snapped his fingers. "That's right!" he said. "Melanie. How could I forget?"

She could tell he was teasing, and it made her tingle with excitement.

"So, I hear all the Mark Twain girls found little red envelopes on their lockers this morning."

Melanie nodded, giving him her best smile.

"I hope you're going to the party," he said earnestly.

"Hmm." Melanie pretended to stall. "I was thinking about it but . . ."

"Laura has great parties," Shane insisted.

The shrill sound of the bell brought their conversation to an abrupt halt. Waving good-bye,

Melanie dashed to her classroom. It would be some party Saturday night, she mused as she dropped into her seat. She just *had* to go.

After school Melanie met her friends at the lockers, and as usual, the talk turned to Laura's party.

"I told Randy that we got invited," Jana said. "He seemed really glad. He said he has to get home early, though, because he's in training for football. The coach wants all the players in bed by ten o'clock every night of the week."

"Terrific!" shrieked Melanie. "That narrows down the amount of time Laura has to work on our guys. I'm glad they're on the football team."

"Hey, wait a minute," said Beth. She gave each of them a horrified look. "I just thought of something. Cheerleading tryouts are Friday after school, and Laura and her friends are going out, too. What if they make it and we don't?"

"Oh, my gosh," said Melanie. "Don't even think about it. I mean, can you imagine Laura on Saturday night if that happened? We wouldn't dare go to the party."

"All I've got to say is, I hope you guys are practicing," said Christie. "Tryouts aren't that far away."

Beth and Jana and Melanie exchanged stricken looks. "Come on, you two," said Melanie. "Let's go to my house and *practice*."

They had just pushed back the furniture in Melanie's family room and lined up to try the hello cheer when the phone rang.

"I get it! I get it!" shrieked Jeffy, who had been peering out from behind the sofa and watching the girls get ready to practice. "Edwards residence. This is Jeffy," he said proudly. He listened for a moment and then turned to his sister. "Melanie, can you come to the phone?"

Melanie sighed. "It never fails," she said in exasperation. "Can you find out who it is?"

Her little brother nodded. "This is Jeffy again," he said importantly. "Who is this, please?" There was a pause. "Garrett Boat?"

"Jeffy!" Melanie shrieked. "Give me that phone!" Then she grimaced. What if he had heard her?

If Garrett had heard her, he didn't let on. "Hi, Mel," he said. "Is it okay if I call you Mel?"

"Sure," she said, beaming at her two friends and giving them a thumbs-up victory sign. "What's up?"

"Not much," he said. "I was just thinking about you and wanted to hear your voice."

"You did? I mean . . . well . . . *great!*" Melanie looked at her friends and blushed. She had never felt so flustered. Especially since he had acted so casual when he saw her in the hall. "I was thinking about you, too."

"Yeah," he went on. "I like your long blond hair. You're awfully cute, you know."

Blond hair? Melanie's lips formed the words but no sound came out. He had said long blond hair. Her hair wasn't blond. It was reddish brown. But in that awful instant she knew who *did* have long blond hair and her heart sank into the pit of her stomach. It was the someone who had been sitting next to her at the soap game and had waved at Garrett at the same time as she had. Just before he asked Christie for her name and phone number. That someone was *Taffy Sinclair.*

"Hey, are you still there?" Garrett asked. "I didn't mean to embarrass you."

"I'm still here," she said quickly, before she could lose her nerve. "It's just that I have to go now. My mom is calling. She needs me for something. I'll talk to you later. Okay?"

"Right," said Garrett, and they hung up.

Melanie stared at the phone. She couldn't turn around and look at her friends. She couldn't even utter a sound. All she could think about was Taffy Sinclair.

It's true, she thought. All this time that he's been calling and talking to me, he's thought I am Taffy Sinclair.

CHAPTER

9

"*W*hat's the matter!" cried Jana.

By this time tears were streaming down Melanie's face. How could Christie have done this to her? Once it got out, she would never be able to face Garrett again. Or Taffy Sinclair. Or the entire student body of Wacko Junior High, for that matter. Between sobs, she explained to Jana and Beth what had happened.

"I think you ought to call Christie," said Beth.

"Me, too," said Jana. "Maybe she can explain it. You know she would never do anything on purpose to hurt you."

Melanie nodded. Beth was right, she thought. There was probably some simple explanation to the whole thing. But what good would that do? another part of her brain argued. Garrett still thought he had been talking to Taffy Sinclair on the phone all this time. What was worse, it was Taffy Sinclair that he WANTED to be talking to.

Picking up the phone, Melanie punched in Christie's number. "Christie?" she said when her friend answered.

"Hi, Melanie. What's up? I thought you and Jana and Beth were going to practice cheers."

Melanie took a deep breath and looked at her two friends for courage. "There's something I have to ask you, and I want you to tell me the truth."

"Sure," said Christie. "You sound so mysterious. Is something wrong?"

Melanie ignored the question. "At the soap game, when Garrett asked you for my name and phone number, was it really me he wanted to know about?"

Christie didn't answer for a moment. When she finally did, her voice was almost a whisper. "Why?"

"Because a few minutes ago he called me again, and he was telling me how cute I am and how much he likes my long blond hair. Long blond hair, Christie. You and I both know who has long blond hair. Taffy Sinclair. And she was sitting next to me at the soap game."

"Oh, Melanie. I'm so sorry. I really did know that Garrett meant Taffy when he pointed up at the crowd and asked me who she was and what her phone number was. But I couldn't stand for Taffy to get him so I told him it was you. Besides, I knew you liked him, and I thought it was a perfect chance for you. You could flirt with him, and he could get to know you. It all happened so fast. I didn't have time to think about what might go wrong, and once I did think about it, it was too late. I'm really sorry. Honest, I am."

"Well, you ought to be!" Melanie blurted. "I don't know what I'm going to do now. I've told *everybody* about Garrett's phone calls and how I thought he liked me. And today I even told Taffy Sinclair that I was responsible for all the Mark Twain girls getting invitations to Laura's party. Oh, Christie, what's going to happen when she finds out the truth?"

"What *are* you going to do?" asked Beth after Melanie had hung up the phone.

Melanie didn't look at her friends for a moment. She was thinking the situation over. She couldn't just hand Garrett over to her old enemy. And of course, she wasn't boy crazy, but on the other hand, Garrett was gorgeous. And she did want him for herself. She put her hands on her hips and slowly faced Jana and Beth, determination shining in her eyes. "Well, I'll tell you one thing, Taffy Sinclair is definitely *not* going to get Garrett Boldt. Not in a million years! So what if this is a case of mistaken identity? It's not my fault. I'm just going to have to impress him with the *real* Melanie Edwards so that when he finds out the truth, he'll forget all about long blond hair, and *Taffy Sinclair.*"

"Way to go, Edwards," said Beth. "Do you still want to practice cheers?"

"Of course I do," said Melanie. "If I'm a cheerleader, I'll have the perfect opportunity to flirt with Garrett at the games. Besides, I'll absolutely die if Taffy makes the squad and I don't."

"Don't forget Laura McCall and her friends," Jana reminded her. "They're trying out, too."

"There's only one problem," Melanie added slowly. "I've got to convince Garrett that it's me he likes before Laura's party Saturday night, because he's bound to find out who's who then."

For the next hour the girls practiced the routines on the sheets Miss Wolfe had given them at the cheerleader meeting on Monday, trying to get all the foot motions, finger snaps, claps, and jumps to fit the right syllables of the cheers.

"This is hard work," Jana complained later as they sat on the floor sipping iced tea and mopping their faces with towels.

"You're telling me," said Beth. "I haven't done splits in ages. The way my thigh muscles are complaining, I'll be lucky if I can walk much less make the squad."

"Oh, come on, Beth," said Melanie. "You're a natural. I was watching you while we were practicing. Jana and I were puffing and groaning, and you were actually *smiling*. You can't wait to get in front of a crowd. It's a cinch that you'll make the squad."

Beth smiled, obviously pleased with the compliment. "I wonder who will make it?" she mused. "I just can't see Taffy out there. She's so prissy. Can you imagine her jumping into the air and screaming 'GO WAKEMAN'?"

"Yeah," said Jana. "She might mess up her hair."

"I think she'll try pretty hard," said Melanie. "Being a cheerleader is awfully important at Wacko. It means instant popularity, especially with the boys. You don't think she'd miss a chance like that, do you?"

"No way," said Beth. "And neither would Laura. What do you bet that she and Tammy are practicing up a storm right this minute?"

Melanie scrambled to her feet. "We can't let her get ahead of us. Come on, guys. Let's PRACTICE."

"Oh, no," groaned Jana. "I don't think I can. I've had it. All I want to do is go home and take a long hot shower."

"Me, too," confessed Beth. "Besides, I'm starved."

After her friends left, Melanie kept on practicing. After a while she closed her eyes, imagining that she was standing on the sidelines in front of the crowd.

The game was almost over, and the Wakeman Warriors were behind by one point. What the team needed was encouragement from the fans. Some spirit! As the players went into a huddle, she ran onto the field alone. She had to do something to save Wakeman from defeat.

"Got the spirit? Let's hear it! Give me a W!" she screamed, punching the air with a fist.

The crowd came to life. "W!" they responded.

"Give me an A!"

"A!" yelled the crowd. They were catching the fever now, and all eyes were on Melanie.

"Give me a K!"

The entire crowd was on its feet, screaming back at Melanie as she stood alone on the field, spelling out W-A-K-E-M-A-N W-A-R-R-I-O-R-S and punctuating the letters with incredible acrobatic feats.

The whistle sounded. Melanie trotted back to the sidelines as the teams took the field again. She held her breath. There were only seconds left in the game. The ball snapped. The Wakeman quarterback handed it off to Scott Daly. Scott paused for an instant, glancing over his shoulder at Melanie. Then with a burst of pure energy he stormed the opposing team's line, crashing through and heading straight down the middle of the field toward the end zone with the ball tucked under his arm. Touchdown! The whistle blew ending the game. Wakeman had won!

Melanie collapsed with relief as she watched Scott head for the sidelines. But he didn't stop once he reached the bench. He headed straight for her.

"Thanks to you, we won!" he shouted. He was glowing with pride as he planted a kiss on her cheek. "It was your cheer that did it. It fired us up just when our spirits were down."

The crowd thundered its agreement and began to chant:

"MELANIE EDWARDS!"

"MELANIE EDWARDS!"

Shane Arrington lifted her into the air and onto his shoulders as the team swarmed around her and joined the chant:

"MELANIE EDWARDS!"

"MELANIE EDWARDS!"

Suddenly Garrett Boldt rushed up and shouted, "Melanie Edwards! You're the one I really like!" Then he began snapping pictures like crazy, capturing it all on film for the yearbook.

Melanie sighed and opened her eyes, but she still saw the crowded football stadium instead of her own family room, and she could just barely hear her mother calling her to dinner over the cheers of the crowd. "I have to make the cheerleading squad," she whispered. "I just *have to*. It could end my boy troubles forever and make all my dreams come true."

CHAPTER

10

*M*elanie awoke the next morning filled with excitement. She couldn't explain why, but she had the feeling that today was going to be her lucky day. She rehearsed the seven tips for flirting as she raced to school fifteen minutes earlier than usual and stationed herself outside the front gate. Scott, Shane, and Garrett all entered the school ground from this direction, and she intended to make the most of it.

Leaning against the chain link fence, she opened her notebook and pretended to be concentrating on her notes. Actually, she didn't even know which subject her notebook was open to because she was trying to see everyone who came up the sidewalk without being obvious about it.

Garrett was the first to appear, sauntering along with his camera slung over his shoulder. It was going to be perfect, *if* she didn't lose her nerve.

Melanie waited until he was even with her, and then she closed her notebook and casually fell into step beside him.

"Oh! Hi!" she said, smiling her very best smile and trying to sound as if she hadn't been aware of his presence until that very instant.

"Hi, back," he said, returning her smile.

At the sight of his dimple, Melanie felt her pulse quicken and her face flush. He was so cute that she almost couldn't stand it. There was no way that she was going to let Taffy Sinclair have him.

Quick, she ordered herself, say something else before he gets away. She tried to remember the tips for flirting that she had been rehearsing just moments before, but her mind was blank. Say anything, she thought. Just get some conversation started.

"I see you have your camera," she said brightly, and then felt instantly foolish. Of course he had his camera. He *always* had his camera. It had been a dumb thing to say. Maybe not as dumb as "I see your nose isn't running," she reasoned, or "I see you're wearing clothes today," but DUMB anyway.

Apparently it hadn't sounded dumb to Garrett because his dimple disappeared as his smile faded.

Then he nodded and said, "Yep, I'm going to shoot some pictures at footbal practice after school. I need to work on getting action shots so that I won't goof up during a real game the way I did at the soap game."

"Oh," Melanie said, and chuckled sympathetically.

He smiled again, too, and called, "See you later," as they entered the gate and he turned to join a group of boys standing nearby.

Melanie wanted to hug herself with joy, but there wasn't time. Instead, she stopped, looked around to make sure no one was watching her, and then put herself into reverse, backing through the gate and into the same spot by the fence where she had waited for Garrett. It was still pretty early and not many kids had arrived yet, so she opened her notebook again and pretended to read.

Her heart had barely stopped fluttering from talking to Garrett when she spotted Scott heading for school. He looked terrific, and his eyes met hers as she peered at him over the top of her notebook.

"Oh! Hi!" she said, trying the same tactic of acting surprised that had worked on Garrett. Still, she felt more relaxed around Scott, and it seemed natural to walk beside him toward school.

"What are you doing here so early?" he teased. "I thought girls always got maximum mirror time in the morning."

Melanie smiled coyly. "Not me. I have more important things to do, like talk to you."

"Great, because I've been planning to talk to you, too. My father is driving me to Laura's party Saturday night. How about if we stop by and pick you up?"

"Super," said Melanie. An image popped into her mind of Laura's opening her door and seeing them standing there together. That ought to give her the message that she can't get away with trying to steal Scott! Melanie had a hard time keeping from laughing out loud. She knew she was grinning from ear to ear, but she didn't even care.

Scott left her at the gate, heading off to look for Randy Kirwan and Mark Peters, and Melanie whirled around and raced back toward her lookout spot, oblivious to everyone around her. For an instant she had caught a quick glimpse of the other members of The Fabulous Five in their regular corner. They had been trying to get her attention. Naturally they would be wondering what on earth she was doing, and she crossed her fingers that they would not come after her.

"Hey, Melody," a familiar voice called out. "Aren't you going the wrong direction? School's the other way."

Melanie skidded to a stop just in time to avoid barreling into Shane. Gasping, she fumbled for words. "Um . . . well . . . I think I dropped a quarter," she offered with a shrug. "Besides, it's *Melanie*, not Melody."

"Oops! Goofed again," he teased. "Okay, *Melanie*, let me help you look for your quarter. Now, where do you think you dropped it?"

She felt her face turning scarlet. She had said another dumb thing. There wasn't any quarter. He would think she was an idiot. Oh, well, she thought. I said it. I'll just have to keep on pretending.

"It could be anywhere along here," she said, ducking her head and looking down toward the ground so that he wouldn't see how badly she was blushing. "Or maybe I didn't drop it, after all. Maybe I left it at home." Melanie giggled nervously. She was supposed to be flirting, she reminded herself, not making up idiotic stories about nonexistent quarters.

"Oh, here it is," said Shane.

Melanie watched in amazement as he reached toward a bare place on the sidewalk, but when he pulled his hand away again, he was holding a quarter.

"How did you do that?" she asked incredulously.

"Do what? Find your lost quarter?"

There was such a gleam in his eye that Melanie couldn't help but burst out laughing as she took the coin and tucked it into her pocket, vowing not to spend it as long as she lived. Shane was laughing, too, and she felt a million times better than she had before.

"That reminds me," he said. "I'm bringing a bunch of terrific tapes to Laura's party. Do you like to dance?"

Melanie felt her eyes growing large. "I love to dance," she said in a whispery voice.

"All right!" said Shane, giving her a thumbs-up victory sign. "It'll be you and me and the tunes on Saturday night!"

Her heart was pounding a crazy beat as she raced to tell the news to her friends. She had been right about this being her lucky day, and what was even better, the day was just beginning.

CHAPTER

11

$\mathcal{M}$elanie walked on air all day. Not only had Scott asked to give her a ride to Laura's party and Shane asked her to dance with him, but Garrett had said that he would be taking pictures at football practice after school. And that had given her a terrific idea.

"Let's go to the football stadium and practice cheers," she suggested when she met Jana and Beth at the lockers after school. "It will be just like cheering at a real game. Besides that, I'll bet nobody else has thought of it. Especially not Laura and Tammy or Taffy Sinclair. It will put us miles ahead of them."

"Isn't the team going to be practicing there?" asked Beth.

"Sure," said Melanie. "So what?"

Jana looked worried. "Do you mean the three of *us* . . . doing cheers in front of *them*?"

"What do you think you'll be doing if you make the squad?" asked Melanie. "Besides, they won't be watching us. The coach will keep them too busy."

"Yeah, but I don't know . . ." said Beth, shaking her head.

"Think about this," Melanie insisted. "We'll know how it feels to do the jumps and cartwheels on grass instead of a gym floor. We'll have a better idea of how to position ourselves in front of the cheering section. We'll look *experienced*. Come on. Let's do it!"

As Jana and Beth reluctantly agreed, Melanie silently congratulated herself on a brilliant idea. It had come to her in a flash as she sat in English class replaying her conversation with Garrett for the millionth time. *I'm going to shoot some pictures at football practice after school,* he had said. Of course Shane and Scott would be there, too. It would be a perfect opportunity to flirt with all three of them again, and a perfect opportunity for them to see her at her best. Besides, she thought with a smile, this was her lucky day.

The gate was open when they arrived at the stadium, but in spite of all of her earlier confidence, Melanie felt suddenly uneasy. It was awfully quiet, and the stadium grounds seemed different without a crowd milling around and the smell of popcorn and hot dogs in the air.

"Are you sure this is okay?" asked Jana.

"I guess there's only one way to find out," she admitted. "Come on. Let's do it."

Melanie led the way as the three girls tiptoed around the end of the stands and along the edge of field. The football team was in the center going through warm-up calisthenics just as they always did before a game. Coach Bledsoe and his two assistants stood to one side holding clipboards and talking among themselves.

"I see Randy," said Jana. "He's in the seventh row, almost in the middle."

As Melanie scanned the rows of players doing jumping jacks, picking out Shane and Scott, Beth was pointing out Keith Masterson. *Oh, no,* Melanie thought, *Shane and Scott are standing next to each other!* How was she going to flirt with one of them without the other one's seeing it? Just then, Shane looked her way and smiled. Melanie hesitated an instant to see that Scott wasn't looking and smiled back.

But where was Garrett? she wondered. He had definitely said he would be here. Without warning, the coach blew his whistle and barked orders to the team. Melanie jumped involuntarily, exchanging nervous glances with her friends.

"Let's put our books on the team bench where we won't trip over them and get started," she said.

"I'm not sure that this was such a great idea," said Jana.

"Why don't we start with a simple sideline cheer?" suggested Melanie, completely ignoring Jana's remark as nervous tingles danced on her scalp. "How about number three on the cheerleading sheet Miss Wolfe gave us?"

They lined up in front of the team bench with Beth on one end, Jana in the middle, and Melanie on the other end, placing their arms and feet in the proper positions for the cheer.

"Go, Warriors, *go*!"

"Fight, Warriors, *fight*!" they began, but Melanie and Jana were repeating the words barely above a whisper.

Beth threw up her arms in disgust and whirled to face her friends. "What's the matter with you two? We're supposed to be cheering, not singing a lullaby."

"I just feel self-conscious," said Jana. "Do you think Coach Bledsoe is looking at us?"

Melanie shot a quick look at the coach, who was turned so that his face was halfway toward them. Even though it had been her idea to practice at the football field, she was fighting her own nervousness. "I don't think so," she said. "Come on, let's get going before we completely lose our nerve."

The girls got back into formation and started the cheer again. This time all three of them yelled at the top of their lungs. The footwork and arm motions were in perfect sync, and they ended the cheer with a gigantic leap into the air.

Applause, punctuated with whistles, broke out behind them. "That was terrific!" Garrett Boldt was standing not ten feet away, camera slung casually over his shoulder, smiling enthusiastically. "You girls are good."

Melanie felt crimson climbing up her face like mercury rising in a thermometer. Even though she had been watching for him, she hadn't known he was there. How had she looked? Had they really been terrific, as he had said?

"Thanks," piped up Beth.

Melanie gave him her best smile. "I'm glad you think so," she said coyly. "We're practicing here so that we'll know how it feels to cheer at a real game. Tryouts are Friday, you know."

"You'll definitely make it," he said. "You three and Melanie Edwards."

Melanie froze. He was talking about Taffy Sinclair! What was happening? Things weren't supposed to work out this way. "What's so special about *her*?" Melanie almost spat out the words, barely hiding her anger.

"Are you kidding?" Garrett asked in amazement. "Take a good look at her. She'll make it, all right."

"There is more to cheerleading than looks," offered Jana. Melanie wanted to hug her. She knew about the mixup, and she was playing along anyway. What a terrific friend, she thought.

"I know that," said Garrett. "I've talked to her lots of times, and she's really nice. But you already know that. She went to Mark Twain with you, didn't she?"

All Melanie could do was nod. She had to change the subject, but how?

"Maybe you could tell me more about her," said Garrett. He was looking straight at Melanie. "You know, her favorites and things like that. I'd really like to get to know her better, especially since we're both going to be at Laura's party Saturday night."

Melanie felt steam rising from under her collar. *Now* what was she going to do? If she told him the truth about Taffy, he'd think she was jealous. And if she lied, he would like Taffy more than ever. Not only that, she wasn't impressing him in the least the way she had planned, because all he wanted to talk about was Taffy Sinclair.

"We'll have to talk about that later," she assured him. "My friends and I have to practice our cheers right now."

Garrett nodded, giving them a friendly smile, and began adjusting his camera. Melanie glanced out to the field where the team had broken into two sections. One was going through passing drills, and the other was working on the tackling dummies on the opposite sidelines. Thank goodness Shane and Scott were too busy to notice her flirting with Garrett, if you could call answering questions about Taffy Sinclair flirting! she thought indignantly.

"Come on," she said, motioning to her friends. "Let's try that sideline cheer again."

"We did that one perfectly," protested Beth. "Let's work on something else."

"Be-*uth*," Melanie said through clenched teeth. "Garrett's watching. I want to do something where I know I'll look good."

Beth shrugged, and the three girls lined up again. Melanie could see out of the corner of her eye that Garrett was looking through the viewfinder of his camera, which was pointed straight at them. Her heart leapt for joy. He was going to practice action shots by taking pictures of them just as she had hoped he would do.

"Go, Warriors, *go*!" they began. Melanie could feel the rhythm building, and she could hear the sound of their voices rising with the spirit of the words. They were doing the cheer more perfectly than before. Garrett couldn't help but be impressed. He would have to see what a great cheerleader she was and forget all about Taffy Sinclair.

Then something went wrong. She would never be able to explain what it was, but she knew it the instant she vaulted into the air for the final leap. Her eyes and mouth both shot open, and she crumpled to the ground with a painful wrench in her left ankle just as she heard Garrett's camera click.

CHAPTER

12

*M*elanie lay paralyzed with embarrassment that blotted out everything happening around her. People were talking, but the first words she understood came from Coach Bledsoe.

"What's going on here?"

Melanie cringed. His voice sounded angry.

"Is she okay? Who gave you girls permission to be out here, anyway?"

"I'm fine! I'm fine!" Melanie insisted, but the moment she tried to get to her feet, she sat down hard again as her ankle refused to support her weight. "Oh, no," she sobbed. "I must have twisted my ankle when I fell."

Tears squirted into her eyes and threatened to roll down her cheeks. I'll die if anyone sees me crying, she thought.

Just then she felt strong arms lift her from the ground. "Let me help you onto the bench," said Scott. He was giving her such a sympathetic look that she almost forgot to hold back the tears. Wonderful Scott, she thought. How could I ever have liked anyone else?

As soon as she was sitting on the bench, Shane knelt in front of her, gently slipping off her sneaker. Then he took her ankle and pressed lightly all the way around it. "Does that hurt?" he asked.

He said it with such concern that Melanie was too choked up to speak. She could only shake her head. She was vaguely aware that her two friends and the rest of the football team had gathered around. Even Coach Bledsoe seemed worried.

"It doesn't look swollen," Shane said. "At least not yet. But maybe we should put an elastic bandage around it anyway."

"Good idea," said Scott, and Coach Bledsoe nodded.

Shane dug around in the team's first aid bag and produced an elastic bandage that he carefully wrapped around her ankle and under her foot. "Now let's see if you can stand up," he said.

Scott and Shane formed a pair of human crutches and gently lifted her to her feet. Melanie knew she was smiling as she put weight on her left foot. She couldn't help it. After her disastrous flirting with Garrett and her klutzy fall doing a cheer, she was now in the arms of two of the handsomest boys in Wacko Junior High!

A cheer went up as she took a step, but Scott and Shane did not let go.

"Look this way with that smile," called out Garrett, and her heart soared even higher as she looked straight into his camera and heard it click. He shot several more pictures as Scott and Shane walked her up and down in front of the bench. He can keep those pictures of me forever, she thought happily.

Finally it was obvious that her ankle wasn't hurt badly, and Coach Bledsoe instructed her on how to use an ice pack to keep the swelling down and then called the team back onto the field. A little later, after the boys were practicing again and Garrett had packed away his camera and left, too, Melanie headed for home with Jana and Beth. The pain was almost gone now, and she had only a slight limp.

"Wasn't that too wonderful for words?" she asked when they stopped in front of her house to say good-bye.

"Wonderful?" snorted Beth. Then she crossed her eyes and made a weird face.

"I understand," said Jana, giving her hand a reassuring squeeze. "See you tomorrow."

The phone rang a few minutes later, interrupting her as she was explaining to her mother about her ankle, putting in every romantic detail.

"It's for you, Melanie," cried out Jeffy, who had beaten her to the phone—as usual.

Melanie hurried to the phone, feeling that if her happiness made her float any higher, she would surely bump her head on the ceiling, but the instant she heard Garrett's voice, she was sure she drifted a couple more inches into the air.

"Hi, Mel," he said softly.

Melanie gulped. The sound of his voice made her feel weak all over. "Hi," she said.

"I'm calling to ask if I can take you home from Laura's party Saturday night," he said.

Melanie closed her eyes and saw red warning lights flashing. He thinks I'm Taffy Sinclair, she reminded herself. I can't say yes. If I do, then when he finds out that I'm not Taffy and that he's stuck taking me home from Laura's party, he'll absolutely *hate* me.

"Mel? Are you still there?" he asked.

"Sure," she said, all the time thinking, I can't say no. This is my big chance with Garrett.

"Please say yes," he insisted. "It would mean a lot to me."

"Yes. I'd love for you to bring me home after the party," she said in a breathless whisper.

It wasn't until after they hung up that Melanie's panic set in. *What on earth am I doing!* she screamed inside her mind. Why did I say yes? But I couldn't say no. Not to Garrett.

She went to her room right after supper to think over the situation. Scott has asked to take her to the party. Shane had asked her to dance with him at the party. And now Garrett wanted to bring her home. It could be the most perfect night of my life, she reasoned.

Then came the objections from the other side of her brain. Scott had been her boyfriend since sixth grade, and it might hurt him to see her with other boys. Shane didn't know anything about Scott or, for that matter, about Garrett. He was so cool and acted so unconcerned all the time that he would probably just drop her flat and never pay attention to her again. And then there was Garrett. So far, her plans for impressing him so that he would forget all about Taffy Sinclair hadn't worked, and he thought Taffy was the one he was taking home Saturday night.

Melanie didn't even hear the phone, so she was surprised when her mother knocked on her door and said she had a call.

"It's another boy," Mrs. Edwards chirped as Melanie took the receiver from her.

Melanie's hand went numb, and she stared at the phone. It was Garrett, she thought frantically. He had found out the truth and was calling to tell her off for tricking him. She couldn't tell him he had the wrong number. He would recognize her voice. I know, she thought. I'll have Jeffy tell him that I can't come to the phone because my ankle is too swollen. Oh, no, she thought. I can't do that. He might be calling for some other reason, and then he'd know I'm not Taffy Sinclair.

She took a deep breath to compose herself and pulled the receiver to her ear. "Hello," she said.

"Hi, Melody. This is Shane . . ." He said something else, but the sound of his voice was lost in rock music punctuated by a hammering sound.

"What!" she shouted. "I can't hear you."

"Just a minute," he shouted back. A few seconds later the music got softer and the hammering stopped. "There," he said. "Can you hear me now?"

"Yes, but what's going on?"

"Not much," he said. "I always entertain Igor at night since he's been by himself all day. He loves for me to play rock music on my stereo, and I tie a pan lid onto his tail so that he can pretend he's a drummer and beat it on the floor in time to the music."

"You're kidding!" screeched Melanie. Then, in spite of herself, she burst out laughing. "This I've got to see."

"Actually, Igor's been practicing for his first public performance, but I doubt if he'll be ready by Saturday night," said Shane. "Anyway, that's not why I called. I was wondering how your ankle feels."

"It's great. I don't think I hurt it badly."

"Super," Shane said. There was real concern in his voice. "I would hate it if you had to miss cheerleading tryouts or . . . the party Saturday night."

They talked for a little while longer, and by the time they hung up, Melanie was feeling so dreamy again that she didn't even remember to remind him that her name was Melanie instead of Melody. Or remember that her boy troubles were only beginning.

CHAPTER

13

*T*he glow she had felt from talking to Shane had worn off by the next morning, and Melanie lay in her bed after the alarm went off thinking about the mess she had gotten herself into.

"Things are totally out of hand," she said out loud. *"Totally!"*

She had three dates for one party, and one of those dates was with a boy who thought she was someone else.

"What am I going to *do-o-o-o*?" she moaned.

She asked the same question of the rest of The Fabulous Five when they met in their special corner of the fence before school.

"You've got to help me," she begged. "At least think up some ideas for how I can get out of this mess. Come on, guys. Think. *Please!*"

Jana's eyes were twinkling. "You could always take a vacation to Abu Dhabi."

"Where's that?" Melanie asked suspiciously.

"Only Asia," said Jana.

"I've got an idea," said Beth. "You could stow away on a steamer to Hong Kong."

"Maybe the next space shuttle flight has an opening," suggested Christie.

"Get serious, you guys," snapped Melanie. "This is important."

"Have you ever thought about not being so boy crazy?" asked Katie.

"I AM *NOT* BOY CRAZY!" she shouted. Why did Katie always say that? It made her furious. "Thanks a lot for *nothing*," she said as she turned and stomped away. I'll show them, she thought. I'll work it out myself.

As she rounded a corner of the school building she almost bumped into Garrett.

"Oh . . . hi," she said, hoping he couldn't see how flustered she was.

"Hi, yourself," he said. "How's that ankle?"

"Oh, it's okay," she said. "It hardly hurts at all this morning."

"Let me show you the pictures I took at football practice yesterday," he said, digging around in his pack. "I developed them last night, and they came out great, if I do say so myself."

Garrett was grinning with pride when he handed her the pictures. Melanie glanced through them, trying to appear casual, and felt a rush of pleasure at how super she looked in every single shot. Then she inspected Shane and Scott, and they looked terrific, too.

"Gosh. Could I have some of these?" she asked.

"I'll make you a set tonight," Garrett offered. "I'd let you have these and make myself a new set except I want to show them to Mr. Neal, the yearbook adviser." Then he added with an embarrassed smile, "He wasn't very impressed with the ones I took at the soap game."

Melanie drifted toward her locker a few minutes later in a total trance. Garrett was starting to like her. She was sure of it. Hadn't he said he would make her a set of pictures so that he could keep those for himself? Sure, he was going to show them to Mr. Neal, but he could have offered to give those to her as soon as Mr. Neal saw them if he didn't want her picture to keep.

But will he still like you if he finds out you're pretending to be Taffy Sinclair? a little voice asked.

I am NOT pretending to be Taffy Sinclair, argued another voice in her mind. *On the phone he calls me Melanie, not Taffy, so how am I supposed to know he has us mixed up?*

You know how, reminded the first voice, *he talked about your blond hair.*

Melanie stared into her locker until the first bell rang, pulling her back to reality. Closing the door and spinning the lock, she turned to head for class and then stopped cold. Taffy Sinclair was at her locker, too, only she wasn't getting her books. She looked especially great in a bright red sweater and she was gazing up into the smiling face of Garrett Boldt!

Melanie cringed and slumped back against her locker. What were they talking about? The party? She peered around Gloria Drexler, who had the locker next to hers, and looked at them again. There was no doubt about it. They were staring into each other's eyes and smiling. Were Garrett's lips moving? Was he telling her how much he liked her blond hair and blue eyes? Her red sweater? Was Taffy nodding? Was she saying she was glad he was taking her home from Laura's party?

Melanie ducked back behind Gloria again as Garrett glanced down the hall in her direction. Her heart was pounding, her pulse racing. Had he seen her? Would he think she was a snoop and a spy?

She waited until Gloria moved away to look at them again, but they were gone. Both of them. It was as if they had disappeared into thin air. In fact, the halls were clearing as kids got their books and headed for class.

Melanie marched to her homeroom like a zombie, trying not to wonder if Garrett had walked Taffy to class. Maybe I'll really hurt my ankle so that I can't go the party, she thought. Or if that doesn't work, maybe I'll fake being sick. Maybe Saturday morning I'll call all three of them and tell them I've been throwing up. No, she thought, I don't want them picturing me barfing up my socks. Surely I'll think of something better between now and then.

Scott was standing outside her homeroom door nervously checking his watch. When he saw her, his face lit up. "Hey, you aren't even limping. That's great," he said. "I tried to call you last night to see how you were, but your line was busy."

"My ankle doesn't hurt anymore," said Melanie. "I guess you took pretty good care of me."

Scott shrugged and turned a bright shade of red. "Well," he said, and Melanie could tell he was fumbling for words. "It's time for the bell. I guess I'd better go." Then he shot off down the hall like a bullet.

For the rest of the morning Melanie couldn't concentrate. Scott really cared about her. He had tried to call last night, but the line had been busy. She cringed. She had probably been talking to Shane. And speaking of Shane, she thought, did she really like him as a boyfriend? Or was she mostly trying to keep him away from Laura McCall? The same went for Garrett. He was gorgeous and older than she was, but was that what really mattered? Or did it have more to do with Taffy Sinclair?

"No," she whispered to herself. "I like all of them."

Sighing, she thought again about the times when no boys ever looked at her. She had been chubby and unattractive then. But things had changed. Changed so much that now there were three boys in her life. It was fun being popular, and with so many cute boys from all over town coming to Wakeman Junior High, how could she help getting carried away?

Carried away. The words echoed in her mind. Was that what Katie meant all those times when she said I was boy crazy? she wondered. Was she trying to warn me about what might happen if I didn't come to my senses?

Laura's party Saturday night could turn into a disaster, thought Melanie, and if that happens, it will be all my fault. Then, in a flash, she knew just what to do.

CHAPTER

14

*I*n the cafeteria at noon all the girls were talking about cheerleading tryouts. It was the last thing in the world that Melanie wanted to think about, even when Alexis and Sara stopped by The Fabulous Five's table.

"I'm not sure I'm going to be ready by tomorrow," said Beth.

"Me either," confessed Alexis. "The cheers seem so easy when I'm practicing them in my head, but when I actually try to do them, I have trouble keeping my hands and feet working in time with the words."

"Me, too," Melanie said absently as she gazed around the lunchroom looking for Scott or Shane. She had made up her mind to be honest. To confess to Shane that she wouldn't be able to dance with him to all the good songs because she would be going to the party with Scott.

"You guys think you're nervous," said Jana. "I can't even eat my cream cheese and jelly sandwich. Not only is tomorrow cheerleading tryouts, but it's the day Mr. Neal announces who will be editors of *The Wigwam*. I really want seventh-grade coeditor badly, and so does Funny. And I *also* want to be a cheerleader."

"We're going to practice after school today, aren't we?" asked Beth. "I mean, we desperately need the practice."

Melanie nodded. She still hadn't been able to spot either of the boys. If only Shane would come in now, before Scott. She would die if he saw her talking to Shane and got jealous.

"Well, I hope we aren't going back to the stadium," said Jana. "Can we go to your house today, Melanie?"

Melanie nodded again just as Sara came up off the bench. "You guys practiced at the stadium?" she shrieked. "Wow! That's cool! Why don't we all go there today and practice together?"

Melanie was just about to tell them about her klutzy fall in front of the entire Wakeman football team, Coach Bledsoe, and Garrett Boldt when she saw Shane coming through the swinging doors. Now was her chance. She had to grab it before she lost her nerve.

"I'll be back in a minute," she said. She didn't even wait for an answer from her friends as she bounded toward the hot-lunch line. Shane had just gotten to the end of the line, and if she hurried, she could step up behind him.

"Oh, Melanie. I need to talk to you." Laura McCall got up from a table and stepped into Melanie's path. "I need to know if any of you girls from The Fabulous Five are coming to my party. You *said* you would let me know as soon as you talked to your mommies and daddies."

Melanie caught the sarcasm. She knew that Laura loved to rub it in that she never had to ask her father permission to do anything the way other kids did. She wanted to tell Laura that she wouldn't be caught dead coming to her party, but of course that wasn't the truth. In fact, it was practically the opposite. She would die if she didn't get to go.

"Sorry," she mumbled. "We'll be there. Seven o'clock. Right?"

"Right," said Laura, flicking her long braid over her shoulder. "Please be on time."

By the time Laura sat down again, Shane was almost to the steam tables, and at least a dozen kids had gotten in line behind him. Melanie chewed on her lip and thought about the situation. If she didn't dance with Shane at the party, maybe he would dance with Laura—to all the good songs—the ones he had asked *her* to dance to. I need to think about this some more, Melanie decided. I'm going to be honest. I swear I am. But not right now.

She saw Shane twice more in the halls during the afternoon, but she still put off talking to him. Instead she thought about Garrett, rehearsing how she would be honest with him, too. She would simply explain that she did not have long blond hair and that she was not whom he thought she was. She wasn't Taffy Sinclair. Still, every time Melanie caught sight of Taffy and thought about Garrett's taking her home and maybe even kissing her good-night, she got an ache in the pit of her stomach.

Alexis, Sara, Beth, and Jana came home with Melanie after school to practice cheers in her family room. She tried hard to keep her mind on cheering. After all, tryouts were tomorrow, but she just could not pay attention, and she always seemed to be one beat behind everyone else.

Once, after the others had landed from a jump before she even left the floor, Jana gave her a sympathetic look and whispered, "What's the matter, Mel? Are you still worrying about your boy troubles?"

Melanie nodded.

"Come on," Jana urged. "Tryouts are tomorrow. Then you still have another whole day until the party. Things will work out by Saturday night. I know they will."

Easy for you to say, Melanie thought. But still, Jana was right about one thing. She still had Friday and most of Saturday to be honest with Shane and Garrett, and just knowing that Jana was sympathetic made her feel so much better that she finished practice with the best cheering she had ever done.

A few times during the evening she made up her mind to go to the phone and call both of the boys, but each time she touched the receiver, she lost her nerve. I'll talk to them at school tomorrow when I can do it face-to-face, she thought, but deep down she knew that it would not be any easier.

The next morning Melanie tried not to look at the spot by the school fence where she had waited for all three boys just two days ago. There's no use waiting there today, she assured herself. They've probably already gone by. Besides, she had to be careful to talk to Shane and Garrett without being seen by Scott.

"Hey, Melody!" a voice shouted behind her.

Melanie froze. It was Shane. She would have to do it now. She couldn't get out of it. Slowly she turned to face him, forcing the corners of her mouth into a smile.

"It's Melanie," she said barely above a whisper.

"Oh . . . *yeah*," he said slowly. "I keep forgetting." Then a smile broke over his face and his eyes began to twinkle so brightly that Melanie knew he was teasing again.

She could almost feel her heart breaking. Shane was so gorgeous and so special. So special, she reminded herself, that she *had* to be honest with him.

"About dancing all the good songs with you at Laura's party . . ." she began.

Shane cocked his head and smiled softly. "You can only dance some of them with me because Scott Daly is taking you to the party."

She gasped. "How did you know?"

"Hey! Scott's my good buddy," he said with a laugh. "We're teammates, remember? I know he's taking you to Laura's, and he knows that I want to dance with you. And do you know what he said to that?" His expression became serious.

Melanie gulped. "No. What?"

Laughing again, Shane said, "He said okay, but not too many dances."

Melanie laughed, too, and she felt almost giddy with relief. As she left Shane and walked on to school a few minutes later, she couldn't help wishing that she could talk to Garrett right then. Quickly. Before the glow from talking to Shane and the good feeling that he hadn't been angry with her had time to wear off.

She wondered later if Garrett had read her mind, because she had no sooner reached the school ground and headed toward The Fabulous Five's special corner of the fence when she saw him coming toward her. He was smiling and waving photographs in his left hand.

"Hi, Melanie. I made these for you last night just as I promised," he said.

She started to reach for the pictures, but her hand stopped in midair. He had called her Melanie! But that was impossible. *He thought she was Taffy Sinclair!*

"You know who I am?" she asked as soon as she could find her voice.

Garrett nodded. "I was showing the pictures to the football team. They said that you were Melanie Edwards and that the blonde in your class is Taffy Sinclair. You know, I was beginning to suspect that something was funny," he added with a puzzled frown. "I would talk to you about something, and then when I mentioned it to Taffy at school the next day, she would act as if she had never heard it before."

Melanie thought she would die. Panic almost choked off her breath. "I didn't know at first that you had us mixed up," she insisted. "Not until a couple of days ago when you said something about my long blond hair. I didn't know what to say . . ."

Her voice trailed off. "So I didn't say anything. Not even when you asked to take me home."

She didn't dare look at Garrett. She had to get it all out before she lost her nerve or fainted or something. "I know you probably think I'm horrible for saying yes. And I'm really sorry, but you won't have to take me home after all."

"I still want to take you home," he said.

Startled, Melanie looked up. Garrett was smiling, and his dimple was even bigger than usual.

"You do?" she asked incredulously.

"Sure. Taffy Sinclair is pretty, but it was you I liked talking to on the phone. Honest! Like I said before, at first I couldn't figure out why she seemed so different in person. Then when I found out who the real Melanie Edwards was, I knew who I really liked." Then he grinned sheepishly and added, "And now that you've been so honest about the mixup, I like you even better."

Part of her wanted to jump up and down for joy, but the other part nagged at her that she hadn't been totally honest yet.

"I like you, too," she said. "But I really can't let you take me home. You see, I'm going to the party with Scott Daly, and it wouldn't be fair not to let him take me home."

"That's okay. I understand," said Garrett. "Things really did get mixed up, didn't they? But you aren't going steady with Scott, are you?"

Melanie's heart fluttered. "No," she said.

"Then maybe sometime we can go to Bumpers for a soda together."

"Terrific!" she said, and she couldn't control the grin on her face as they parted. Being honest had never felt so super! But that wasn't all. Even though it was great to be liked for her looks, it was even *better* to be liked for the kind of person she was.

CHAPTER

15

$\mathcal{M}$elanie had never been so nervous in her life. Before Jana, Beth, and she went into the gym for cheerleader tryouts, Christie and Katie gave them big hugs. Now the three of them were clustered near the doorway, nervously rehearsing cheers in their minds and watching other seventh-graders file in.

"This is it!" said Beth, dancing around on tiptoes.

"I'm really worried," confessed Jana. "I just can't seem to get some of the routines down. *Plus*, Mr. Neal is posting the list of yearbook editors right this minute, and I won't be able to find out if I made it until after tryouts."

Even though Melanie felt better about Shane and Garrett and had been congratulated by all of her friends for her honesty, she couldn't help wishing she had practiced the cheers a little bit harder. "At least I won't be first," she mumbled.

"E-gad!" shrieked Beth. "I might be. Barry. That's near the front of the alphabet." Beth scanned the growing crowd in the gym. "Oh, good. I forgot all about Dekeisha Adams," she said, pointing to a tall black girl talking to friends on the other side of the room.

Just then Miss Wolfe entered, and everyone got quiet.

"Good afternoon, ladies. Ve vill begin the tryouts in just one moment." Then she instructed them to line up in alphabetical order in front of the bleachers and to come forward one at a time, introducing themselves and then doing their favorite cheer from the sheets she had passed out. Across the room at a long table sat four judges: Miss Zimmerman, the music teacher; Mrs. Strizak, the gymnastics coach from the Y; and two varsity cheerleaders, ninth-grader Kaci Davis and eighth-grader Colby Graham.

After everyone was lined up, Miss Wolfe sat down in the fifth judge's chair. "Ve are now ready to begin," she said, nodding to Dekeisha Adams.

The next few minutes were a blur as Melanie waited for her turn to come. Her heart was pounding so loudly she could barely hear the other contestants' cheers. But she could see that Dekeisha was fantastic, and so was Beth. Heather Clark was good, and Alexis, and the next thing she knew it was her turn.

Melanie sprang to the center of the floor and introduced herself to the judges. Then she took a deep breath and got into position for her cheer. She had chosen the same one she had yelled in her dream, that fantastic dream where she had inspired the team to victory and the crowd had chanted her name in thanks.

"Got the spirit? Let's *hear it*!" she screamed. "Give me a W!"

Silence. For an instant she was stunned. Then suddenly she realized why. This was tryouts. There was no crowd to return her cry. Closing her eyes quickly, she pictured the crowd and heard them scream "W" back to her.

"Give me an A!" she yelled. Again, her make-believe audience responded. By the time she had spelled out W-A-K-E-M-A-N W-A-R-R-I-O-R-S and finished with a double somersault, her imaginary crowd was on its feet roaring.

Melanie opened her eyes. The judges were all smiling, and she raced back to her place in line on legs that were almost crumpling beneath her from relief.

She tried to watch the rest of the girls go through their routines. Melinda Thaler tripped going onto the floor, and Jana forgot her routine halfway through and had to start over, but most of the girls were good. Taffy Sinclair was prissy, as usual, but Melanie could tell that the judges liked her. It was obvious that they liked Laura McCall and Tammy Lucero, too.

After everyone had finished, Melanie fidgeted as the judges marked their score sheets. There were only eight positions on the squad. She would die if she didn't get one of them.

Finally Miss Wolfe stood, picking up a piece of paper and holding up her hand for silence. "Here are the names of the seventh-grade girls who will form the junior varsity cheerleading squad. De-keisha Adams, Beth Barry, Alexis Duvall, Melanie Edwards, Tammy Lucero, Laura McCall, Mandy McDermott, and Taffy Sinclair. Congratulations, girls, and thank you to everyone else who tried out."

Melanie was so excited that she thought she would burst. She began jumping up and down and shrieking with the other seven girls who had made the squad. It wasn't until she and Beth were jumping and giggling together that a terrible thought hit her. It must have struck Beth at the same instant because both girls froze and stared at each other.

"Jana," whispered Melanie.

"She didn't make it," said Beth. "Where is she?"

They looked first among the crowd of sad-faced girls who were leaving the gym, but Jana wasn't among them. She wasn't in the middle of the winners and friends who were congratulating them, either.

"Oh, my gosh," said Melanie. "Where could she be? I feel terrible."

"So do I," said Beth. "I was so excited about making the squad that I completely forgot about her. I'll bet she's crushed. She wanted to make cheerleader as much as we did. I hope she didn't think we deserted her and then went away somewhere to cry."

Just then Melanie noticed someone trying to push her way into the gym through the crowd that was leaving. "Look!" she cried. "It's Jana. And she's *smiling*!"

"I made it! I made it!" Jana cried as she rushed toward them, her face aglow. "And so did Funny Hawthorne. We're going to be seventh-grade co-editors of the yearbook."

"Wow! That's great," said Melanie. "We couldn't find you, and we were worried."

"Sorry," said Jana. "And congratulations to you guys for making the squad. When I found out I didn't, I just had to duck out and check *The Wigwam* staff. You know," she added thoughtfully, "it's a good thing I'm not going to be a cheerleader. Yearbook is going to take up a lot of time."

Laughing, Melanie grabbed her two friends' arms and together they skipped out of the gym.

CHAPTER

16

*T*his was it. Laura McCall's party. Melanie stood in front of her mirror surveying herself. She had tried on everything in her closet before choosing her best white jeans and a turquoise sweater that set off her burnished hair. What would Laura wear? Something terrific, probably. And how would she treat The Fabulous Five? At least there would be lots of kids there. Maybe they could just blend in.

Mr. Daly dropped off Melanie and Scott at the apartment building where Laura lived. It was easy to find Laura's apartment. The door to #7 was wide open and music was coming from inside. Melanie shivered nervously until she noticed other kids entering the building behind them.

Just as they walked through the door, a tall, handsome man with blond hair stepped up and stuck out his hand. "Hi, there," he said. "I'm Laura's father. It looks as if I got home from Atlanta just in time for a party."

Melanie pretended to cough to hide a giggle while Scott shook Mr. McCall's hand. So this party is going to be chaperoned after all, she thought with a smile.

The living room was crowded with kids and more were pouring in the door all the time. She knew practically everyone there: most of the cheerleading squad, a few eighth-graders, and even a couple of kids from Copper Beach in addition to Riverfield and Mark Twain kids.

Laura was standing in one corner with Tammy and Melissa, looking frustrated and shooting poison-dart looks at the back of her father's head. It was obvious that she had primped extra hard for this party because she looked gorgeous in a pale blue jumpsuit. Jana and Randy were nearby, talking to Funny. Probably about the yearbook, thought Melanie. So far, so good. Maybe this party would be all right, after all.

She was watching for Shane and Garrett, but neither of them had arrived yet. Scott brought her a soda just as Beth, Christie, and Katie popped in the door together and waved in their direction.

As Melanie raised her hand to wave back to her friends, Taffy Sinclair stepped into the room wearing a pale blue jumpsuit that was identical to the one Laura wore. She had probably meant to make a grand entrance, but a few girls gasped, and everyone else got quiet as Taffy and Laura stared in horror at each other. Neither girl moved a hair as anger gleamed in their eyes.

"Hey!" shouted Curtis Trowbridge. "Twins!"

That broke the tension for everyone except Taffy and Laura. Melanie watched as they carefully turned their backs to each other and pretended the other one did not exist while everyone else started talking again and a few couples danced. Melanie and Scott danced several times, and she even danced with Garrett when he arrived a little while later.

"Where's Shane?" she whispered to Jana. "The party has been going on for an hour, and he's still not here?"

"I haven't heard anything about him not coming," said Jana. "Maybe he's sick, or something."

"Not Shane," Melanie assured her. Then her face brightened and she burst out laughing as Shane came through the door leading an iguana on a leash.

"Meet Igor," he called out as kids squealed and pointed toward the lizard. Igor seemed unperturbed by the crowd and as cool as Shane, looking around and flicking his tongue first to the right and then to the left.

"Is he going to play the drums for us?" asked Melanie.

"Naw," said Shane, giving her a wink that made her heart flutter. "I brought him along so that he could dance with me to all the good tunes."

The rest of the party was terrific, including the food, which was a ten-foot-long submarine sandwich cut in sections and served with chips and brownies. Garrett shot pictures all over the place, getting several of Melanie. Everyone talked and danced and had a good time, except for Laura and Taffy, who spent the evening making a big deal of ignoring each other. And by time to go home, almost everyone had gotten up the nerve to pet Igor at least once.

"It was a great party, wasn't it?" Melanie asked Scott as Mr. Daly drove them home.

"Yeah," said Scott. "It sure was."

And then, when he walked her to the door, he pulled her behind an evergreen bush and kissed her.

Melanie stood watching Scott drive away. She felt so dreamy she could barely stand it. Just think, she told herself, Scott really likes me, and I came so close to messing up a good thing.

She said good-night to her parents and went to her room. Still, she thought as she got ready for bed and Shane's and Garrett's faces reappeared in her mind. Scott and I aren't going steady, and Shane and Garrett are awfully cute. Maybe it wouldn't hurt to keep on flirting with them once in a while.

She sighed, knowing what Katie would say. She'll say I'm boy crazy, thought Melanie. Then she hugged herself and smiled.

So, let her. Being a *little bit* boy crazy is fun!

CHAPTER

17

On Monday morning Christie got up before anyone else in her family and tiptoed outside to get the morning newspaper. She couldn't wait until breakfast to read her horoscope. Not that she believed in such things, of course, but her horoscope for Saturday had said that a mysterious stranger would enter her life. That had to have meant Jon Smith. She had thought he was cute ever since school started, but Saturday night at Laura's party she had caught him looking at her from across the room three times.

She sighed and smiled to herself as she leafed through the paper looking for the horoscope page. So what if most kids say he's boring? He's just quiet, she thought, that's all. I'm quiet, myself. And so what if his parents are big deals on the local television station? Celebrities, actually. It's wrong the way some kids butter him up just to get to meet his parents.

In a way, she knew how he felt. Sometimes kids tried to take advantage of the fact that Mr. Bell, the principal of Wakeman Junior High, was a friend of her parents. So what? she thought. That had nothing to do with Saturday night and Jon Smith's looking at her *three whole times*!

Finally she found the horoscope and looked down the list of signs until she found her own:

Aquarius (Jan. 20–Feb. 18) Your best qualities push you into the limelight. Special meeting will bring either conflict or romance. You could find yourself under pressure. Beware!

Christie read over the message at least a dozen times. The parts about conflict and pressure made her shiver, but what was the meaning of the special meeting that could bring romance? Did that mean that she would actually come face-to-face with Jon? And why would she have to "beware"? Find out in *The Fabulous Five #3: The Popularity Trap.*

ABOUT THE AUTHOR

Betsy Haynes, the daughter of a former news-woman, began scribbling poetry and short stories as soon as she learned to write. A serious writing career, however, had to wait until after her marriage and the arrival of her two children. But that early practice must have paid off, for within three months Mrs. Haynes had sold her first story. In addition to a number of magazine short stories and the Taffy Sinclair series, Mrs. Haynes is also the author of *The Great Mom Swap,* and its sequel *The Great Boyfriend Trap.* She lives in Colleyville, Texas, with her children and husband, who is the author of a young adult novel.

YOUR OWN

SWEET VALLEY HIGH®

SLAM BOOK!

If you've read *Slambook Fever*, Sweet Valley High #48, you know that slam books are the rage at Sweet Valley High. Now *you* can have a slam book of your own! Make up your own categories, such as "Biggest Jock" or "Best Looking," and have your friends fill in the rest! There's a four-page calendar, horoscopes and questions most asked by Sweet Valley readers with answers from Elizabeth and Jessica

It's a must for SWEET VALLEY fans!

☐ 05496 FRANCINE PASCAL'S SWEET VALLEY HIGH
SLAM BOOK
Laurie Pascal Wenk $3.50

- -

GOOD NEWS! The five best friends who formed the AGAINST TAFFY SINCLAIR CLUB will be starring in a series all their own.

IT'S NEW. IT'S FUN. IT'S FABULOUS. IT'S THE FABULOUS FIVE!

From Betsy Haynes, the bestselling author of the Taffy Sinclair books, *The Great Mom Swap*, and *The Great Boyfriend Trap*, comes THE FABULOUS FIVE. Follow the adventures of Jana Morgan and the rest of THE FABULOUS FIVE as they begin the new school year in Wakeman Jr. High.

☐ SEVENTH-GRADE RUMORS (Book #1)

The Fabulous Five are filled with anticipation, wondering how they'll fit into their new class at Wakeman Junior High. According to rumors, there's a group of girls called The Fantastic Foursome, whose leader is even prettier than Taffy Sinclair. Will the girls be able to overcome their rivalry to realize that rumors aren't always true? 15625-X $2.75

☐ THE TROUBLE WITH FLIRTING (Book #2)

Melanie Edwards insists that she *isn't* boy crazy. She just can't resist trying out some new flirting tips from a teen magazine on three different boys—her boyfriend from her old school, a boy from her new school, and a very cute eighth-grader! 15633-0 $2.75/$3.25 in Canada

☐ THE POPULARITY TRAP (Book #3)

When Christie Winchell is nominated for class president to run against perfect Melissa McConnell from The Fantastic Foursome, she feels pressure from all sides. Will the sudden appearance of a mystery candidate make her a winner after all? 15634-9 $2.75

HER HONOR, KATIE SHANNON (Book #4)

When Katie Shannon joins Wakeman High's new student court, she faces the difficult job of judging both her friends and foes. On Sale: December 15640-3 $2.75

Watch for a brand new book each and every month!

Book #5 On Sale: January/Book #6 On Sale: February

Buy them at your local bookstore or use this page to order:

Bantam Books, Dept. SK28, 414 East Golf Road, Des Plaines, IL 60016

Please send me the books I have checked above. I am enclosing $_____ (please add $2.00 to cover postage and handling). Send check or money order—no cash or C.O.D.s please.

Mr/Ms _____

Address _____

City/State _____ Zip _____

SK28—11/88

Please allow four to six weeks for delivery. This offer expires 5/89.